ANIMAL

Special two-in-one edition

Kittens in the Kitchen
Bunnies in the Bathroom

Animal Ark series

LUCY DANIELS

Kittens
— *in the* —
Kitchen

Illustrations by Shelagh McNicholas

Hodder
Children's
Books

a division of Hodder Headline plc

This edition of Kittens in the Kitchen and Bunnies
in the Bathroom first published in 1998.
ISBN 0 340 74665 3
**Special thanks to C. J. Hall, B.Vet.Med., M.R.C.V.S.
for reviewing the veterinary information contained in this book**

Kittens in the Kitchen
**To Jenny Oldfield, who loves animals, and to
Peter and Benjamin, the kittens in my kitchen.**

Text copyright © by Ben M. Baglio 1994
Created by Ben M. Baglio
London W6 0HE
Illustrations copyright © by Shelagh McNicholas 1994

First published as a single volume in Great Britain in 1994
by Knight Books (now Hodder Children's Books)

The right of Lucy Daniels to be identified as the Author of
the Work has been asserted by her in accordance with the
Copyright, Designs and Patents Act 1988.

10 9 8 7 6 5 4 3 2 1

A catalogue record for this book is available from the British Library

Typeset by Avon Dataset Ltd, Bidford-on-Avon

Printed and bound in Great Britain by Clays Ltd, St Ives plc

Hodder Children's Books
A division of Hodder Headline plc
338 Euston Road, London NW1 3BH

To Jenny Oldfield, who loves animals, and
to Peter and Benjamin, the kittens in my kitchen

One

'Mandy, you're very keen on school all of a sudden,' Mr Hope said. He watched her stuff old newspapers into her schoolbag. She flung on her school jacket, flicked a brush through her dark blonde hair and snatched a mouthful of toast. 'It's only ten to eight. Are you sure you're OK?'

'Very funny!' Mandy said. 'Of course I'm OK. It's just a special day, that's all.' She'd fed her rabbits and done her morning chores at Animal Ark. Simon, the nurse, had come in to take over care of the animals and do temperatures and medicines. Now she was free to go.

'School trip?' Mr Hope took a guess as Mandy unlocked her bicycle padlock and put on her crash-helmet. He got no reply. 'New boyfriend?'

'Ha, ha!' Mandy said. 'No time now, Dad. I'll tell you later.' She set off up the front drive, her long legs pedalling like mad. She waved at her mother.

'What's the rush?' Mrs Hope wound down her car window.

But Mandy had already sped by, under the wooden sign, 'Animal Ark, Veterinary Surgeon'. She took one look back at the old stone cottage with its modern vets' extension to the rear, then she pedalled hard again. Her heavy schoolbag dragged across her shoulder.

'She's up to something,' Mandy heard Mrs Hope say. 'She's got that determined look on her face.'

Mandy knew they wouldn't have a clue what she wanted with the old newspapers. But she ignored them and charged up the lane towards Welford village. She'd keep her mystery until evening, after Mrs Hope came back from her round of visits to the sick cats, dogs, goats and hamsters that made up the busy practice of Animal Ark. She gave her mum and dad one last wave before she turned out on to the road. 'See you later!' she yelled.

*   *   *

'This is it! This is the big day!' Mandy greeted her friend, James Hunter. As usual, his straight brown hair flopped on to his forehead, and his glasses sat halfway down his nose.

'Hi,' he said. 'Do you realise I've dragged myself out of bed half an hour early to meet up with you outside this rotten post office!' He was breathless from pedalling. 'My dad nearly dropped dead with shock!'

'Come on!' Mandy said, ignoring his protests, 'Let's go and see!'

Mandy and James cycled out of Welford on the two mile stretch into Walton. Past all the sleepy cottages and wide awake farms with their collie dogs at the gate, she never once stopped chattering.

'It's going to be today, I know it!' She had a feeling about these things. James nodded and panted to keep up. 'I'm so excited, I can hardly wait!' The ground sped by under their wheels. 'She's been looking for a warm dry place, and that's always a sign! Anyway, she refused her food yesterday.' James nodded again in agreement. 'I did see her in the caretaker's porch yesterday after school, behind the stack of logs. She's a very clever cat!'

They pedalled down the final hill. Mandy's short hair blew back in the wind. The new bungalows of

Walton greeted them, spick and span. Walton Moor School lay behind these new houses; another new building which backed on to open countryside. Mandy and James rode through the gateway into the deserted playground.

Mr Williams, the caretaker, strode through the grounds, setting out parking cones for the dustbin lorry. It was Thursday, bin day. 'Morning!' Mandy called, with James running to catch up. But Mr Williams was a man of few words. He ignored her greeting.

'Shh, now!' Mandy warned James. They'd left their bikes locked up in the shed, and came up behind the caretaker's house. 'We don't want to disturb her.' Carefully they peered over the beech hedge, neatly trimmed by Mr Williams. They scanned his pink rose bushes and the porch at the back of his house.

'Mandy,' James dared to whisper, 'does Mr Williams know about this?' He was cleaning his glasses on his school jumper. 'I mean, what will he say if he finds us snooping about on his porch?'

'He won't mind,' Mandy whispered back. How could anyone mind about animals? 'Mrs Williams sometimes puts out food. I expect that's why Walton has chosen their porch to have her babies in!'

Mandy's face shone with excitement.

'Walton?' James didn't realise the cat had a name. It was small, black and white and rather ordinary. As far as he knew, it was a stray. But then Mandy had kept details about the cat pretty much to herself up till now.

'I named her after the school,' Mandy said. 'According to Mrs Williams, she just turned up on the main doorstep one night, dumped inside a plastic bag, with tiny airholes to breathe through. Can you believe it? People can be so cruel!'

Mandy could feel the prick of tears in her eyes even now. 'She was only a young cat and someone just dumped her!' She sniffed and tried to pull herself together. 'She would've died if I hadn't come along early next morning and gone to the staffroom for some milk for her. She was really neglected. I had to feed her up.' She squared her shoulders. 'Anyway, that was six weeks ago. She's the school cat now, only a sort of half stray. So it's up to us to look after her!'

With that, Mandy eased open the back gate into the Williams's garden. 'Walton! Walton!' she coaxed, bending low and looking under the stilted porch into the dark space there. James peered up on to the porch itself, behind the stack of logs. No cat.

'Walton!' Mandy called, a bit more loudly.

A black and white shape trotted across the long shadows of the lawn, and over the flower-bed; a round, heavy shape, nearly as wide as she was long, with a low belly. James spotted her first. 'Mandy, look!' he said.

Mandy breathed a sigh. They'd got here in time. 'Hello, Walton,' she said. 'Here's a nice, comfy place for you to give birth to your lovely kittens, see!' She climbed the porch steps. The cat followed. Mandy delved into her bag and drew out the old newspapers. She showed them to Walton and let her sniff them. 'See, nice and warm and dry!'

Then she and James banked up some of the logs to make a sort of den for Walton. They lined it with the newspapers, carefully overlapping them in thick layers. 'See!' Mandy said again.

Walton brushed against Mandy's bare legs. She tilted her head up towards the special bed of logs and newspapers. Her delicate nose and whiskers seemed to approve, for she climbed, slow and heavy, up on to the ledge.

'It's in the sun, nice and warm,' James said. 'Good idea!' He grinned at Mandy then blushed. In the distance, the morning bell sounded. 'Was that the bell?' he asked clumsily. Then he shot off for registration before Mandy could reply.

'You hear that, Walton?' Mandy said. 'That's the bell. I have to go.' But she felt the strong pull that the cat had over her. Perhaps it was because she, Mandy Hope, aged thirteen, of Animal Ark, Welford, Yorkshire, was very like Walton, the school cat. They were both adopted. Her own parents had died in a car crash, too early for her to remember them, and Adam and Emily Hope had taken her in. Now she would do the same for Walton.

Softly she stroked the cat, then she caught hold of herself. 'I'll stop fussing now and leave you to cope.' She knew animals liked privacy at this time. 'No one will bother you, and I'll be back later to see how you've got on.' Quietly she backed down from the porch, then quickly she cut across the garden, through the gate and over the tarmac of the playground. The second bell had gone.

Mr Williams, in his padded green waistcoat, his old corduroy trousers and his big laced boots, crossed paths with Mandy as she ran into school through the main door. As usual, he only grunted, head down and grumpy. Mandy thought it was best not to say anything to him about Walton and her arrangements for the birth. Leave it till later. Even Mr Williams's heart would melt once he saw Walton's kittens nestling on his back porch!

Mandy rushed into lessons. She tried, and failed, to concentrate all the way through maths, geography and English.

At half past three James was waiting for Mandy at the lockers. 'Ready?' he asked. Like Mandy, animals were the most important thing in James's life.

Dodging the crowds, they sprinted together up the slope to the caretaker's house. Mandy could hardly breathe for excitement. This was Walton's big day!

'Walton!' Mandy called, easing the gate, crossing the lawn. They turned the corner up on to the porch. Mandy half closed her eyes. There Walton would be, tucked up in her newspaper bed, shielding her new kittens! She couldn't wait!

She opened her eyes. The bed was empty! Clean and dry and quite empty. Mandy looked at James. They felt the bottom of the world fall out.

'Where is she?' James gasped.

Mandy shook her head. 'It's today. I'm sure it's today.' She couldn't understand it. She'd seen enough cats giving birth to kittens at Animal Ark to know just how they looked when the great day came. Mandy and James stood on the porch, confused and alarmed.'

'Listen!' Mandy said. The Williamses' back door

stood open in the afternoon sunshine, and Mandy was sure she'd picked up a sound from inside. A tiny, high-pitched squeaking sound!

James stared at her. 'What is it?'

Mandy stepped across the kitchen threshold. 'Mr Williams?' she whispered. 'Mrs Williams?'

The kitchen was neat and clean, scrubbed to perfection. Its lace curtains shone pure white. Its black and white tiles looked like an advertisement for floor cleaner. But it was empty. The squeaking noise was slightly louder. 'In here!' Mandy said.

They tiptoed into the empty room.

'It's still very muffled,' James said. He looked inside cupboards, trying to find the noise.

They looked under shelves, behind the vegetable rack, but still the noise escaped them.

'Walton!' Mandy called gently.

But Walton, wherever she was, didn't want company. Only the muffled, faint squeaking continued. Mandy followed it until she finally tracked it down.

There was a linen basket in the corner of the kitchen, by the washing-machine. It was an old-fashioned straw one with a lid. Mandy put her ear to it. The squeaking came from inside!

Gingerly she lifted the lid. It was dark and warm in

there. The high-pitched noise rose to a wailing chorus. Mandy adjusted her eyes to the darkness and peered inside. She saw the black and white patches of Walton's fur, she saw the cat's eyes glint as she looked up. Obligingly, Walton lifted a paw and shifted sideways. 'Look!' she seemed to be saying, 'Four perfect kittens!'

Mandy could just make them out; four tiny curled up things, grey and blind. Skinny, helpless creatures. She thought they were the most beautiful things she'd ever seen!

'Aren't they wonderful!' Mandy breathed, as James came to look over her shoulder.

He saw their blunt little faces and blind eyes. 'Ye-es,' he said. He clearly needed more time to get used to them.

'Oh, but they are!' Mandy cooed. She touched Walton gently under the chin. 'Clever girl!' she said. The kittens squeaked louder in protest at the light and the cooler air. Mandy gave in and replaced the laundry basket lid.

And then their luck ran out. Someone crossed the porch and filled the kitchen doorway. He was tall, bulky, and his feet made a noise across the wooden floor of the porch. 'Amy?' he called. He paused, wiped his feet, then stepped into the kitchen.

'Mr Williams! Um, hello!' Mandy said feebly. James stood alongside her, straightening his school tie, trying to look braver than he felt.

'What the heck!' Williams bellowed with shock. 'Amy! Where are you? What the heck!' he said again.

His wife came pottering through from the front room. She was slightly deaf, slightly short-sighted. 'Don't shout, Eric,' she sighed. 'I can hear perfectly well without you having to shout!'

'Oh, can you?' her husband fumed. 'I expect you heard these two prowling around in here perfectly well, too!'

Mrs Williams sighed again. 'Sit down all of you,' she said. 'Everybody sit down while I make us a cup of tea!' It was clearly her cure for everything.

Mandy and James sat down as they were told, as far away from Mr Williams as possible, while his wife made the tea. 'Well!' he said over and over. 'Can't a man even call his house his own any more?'

'Oh, shush, Eric!' his wife said, giving him his favourite mug and a Rich Tea biscuit. 'Just give them a chance to explain!' She was little and skinny, half his size, but Mandy and James could see who was boss. 'Well, then,' Mrs Williams smiled sweetly

at Mandy. 'I'm sure there's a perfectly good explanation!'

'There is,' Mandy agreed. She looked wildly at James for help.

'The cat's had kittens!' James blurted out.

'In your laundry basket,' Mandy finished off.

'What!' Mr Williams shot to his feet. He backed off into a corner.

'Wait!' Mrs Williams went to investigate. She lifted the basket lid and peered inside. 'It has,' she confirmed calmly. 'It's had kittens all right.'

'On my best shirts!' Mr Williams stammered. 'It's had kittens on my best shirts!'

'Calm down, Eric!' Mrs Williams shook her head. 'It's only a stray cat!'

'Only!' The caretaker rolled his eyes in helpless anger.

'She won't do any harm,' Mandy broke in. 'They're very clean animals. She won't leave any mess!' She tried to reason with him. 'If you just leave her and the kittens in peace in there for a few days, they'll soon be on their feet. Then you can make them a better place; a cardboard box, for instance. Just line it with newspaper and put it out on the porch. That should be fine!'

'A few days!' Mr Williams repeated. His face seemed to be stuck. His mouth had dropped open, his eyes were bulging.

Mrs Williams took Mandy and James to one side. She shook her head. 'It's no use. He can't stand them.'

Mandy was slow to catch on. 'Can't stand what?' Only now was she beginning to sense there was a problem.

'Cats. He can't stand them. They set his nerves on edge.'

Mandy breathed in deeply. How could people hate cats?

'He says they dig up his garden. He can't abide

them.' Mrs Williams sounded sorry, but she sounded as if they'd just have to understand. Her husband was stubborn as a mule over cats. She turned and started clearing away the tea things.

'Just a few days!' Mandy said, dashing from one to the other. 'We can't move them for a few days in case the mother decides to abandon the kittens. She might do if they get moved. Please let her stay where she is!' She felt breathless with fright, but she tried not to show it.

'Stay? In my linen basket!' Mr Williams snorted. 'On my best shirts!' He tossed his head. 'A load of smelly cats!'

'They're not—' Mandy interrupted, but James stopped her. He had a better idea of when to answer back than Mandy.

'Not likely!' Mr Williams headed straight at Mandy and James to shoo them out of his kitchen. 'Go on, you two. Look sharp! I shan't warn you again!'

Mandy and James backed off towards the door. Mr Williams towered over them. 'Please!' Mandy pleaded. She felt sick at heart.

'No!' Mr Williams thundered. 'They've got to go!' He glanced at his wife. 'And there's no use you looking like that, Amy, so you can just pipe down!

I'm saying no and I mean no!' He looked down at Mandy's terrified face. 'I'm telling you once and for all, I'm not having them kittens in my kitchen!'

Two

Mr Williams said his final word then stormed out of the room. Tears sprang to Mandy's eyes. She looked in desperation at Mrs Williams.

The old woman raised her eyebrows and rolled her eyes. She patted her neat grey hair. 'Just give him a minute to cool down,' she said. She lifted the linen basket lid to take a peek for herself. 'My, my,' she murmured.

'He can't mean it,' Mandy said to James, who was trying to drag her out of the kitchen on to the back porch. 'He can't just sentence four perfectly harmless kittens to death, can he? It isn't fair!'

James shook his head and kept on pulling. 'Come on, we'd better go!'

'Mrs Williams!' Mandy pleaded.

The caretaker's wife carefully washed up the rose-patterned teacups. She put them away in a high, glass-fronted cupboard. 'I'm saying nothing,' she said steadily.

Mandy shook herself free of James. 'But it isn't fair, is it? I mean, what have those poor little kittens ever done to anybody? They deserve a chance to live, just like anyone else! You can't just chuck them away because they happen to have been born in an unusual place!'

'On top of my husband's best shirts,' Mrs Williams reminded her. 'My Eric's very particular about his shirts.' She turned to face Mandy, who was head and shoulders taller, but thin as a piece of string. 'Anyhow, whoever said life was fair?'

'But if he moves them, they'll die! Walton will abandon them!' Again the tears pricked her eyelids.

Mrs Williams stared up at her. 'Walton?' She folded her arms and kept her gaze steady.

'The mother cat. I've called her Walton after the school. I wanted her to sound as if she belonged somewhere! As if she was looked after, and had a home, and somebody who cared!' Mandy rushed on.

The tears were rolling down her cheeks now. They ran with a salty taste into her mouth. She remembered the half-starved cat being dumped in the school doorway. She thought of herself. What would have happened to her if Emily and Adam Hope hadn't taken her in and cared for her when she was tiny?

'Mandy!' James whispered. 'Don't cry. You see worse things than this at the Ark every day of the week, remember.'

'No, let her alone,' Mrs Williams said thoughtfully. 'She's right. They deserve a chance.' She took Mandy by the hand and sat her down at the table. Late afternoon sun filtered in through the white net curtains. 'But for goodness sake, dry your eyes, young woman. I can hear my Eric coming back across the yard, and he can't abide waterworks!' She pulled a clean handkerchief out of her apron pocket and handed it to Mandy. 'Quick, blow your nose!'

'Will you help us?' Mandy whispered. The caretaker's big boots tramped up the steps and across the porch. 'If you let the kittens stay, I'll come here every day, twice a day, to help look after them! I'll—'

'Shush!' Mrs Williams warned. Her husband hung his cap on the door peg. She stood up and leaned forward evenly, with clenched fists down on the table.

'What the — !' Mr Williams's face darkened as he caught sight of Mandy and James. 'I thought I'd told you to clear off! What's the matter, are you deaf?'

'Now, Eric,' Mrs Williams began steadily.

'Don't you "now, Eric" me!'

'Now, Eric!' she insisted. 'This young girl has been explaining to me again about these kittens being moved. It seems the mother won't have any more to do with them if we interfere. They've to be left alone.'

A loud miaow of agreement from inside the basket backed up the end of Mrs Williams's firm speech. Thin squeaks followed after in a kind of chorus. Mr Williams paced up and down the kitchen.

'Stand still, Eric, and listen!' Hands on hips, the tiny woman in the flowery apron confronted her heavyweight husband. 'Where's the harm in it? You've a drawer full of shirts up those stairs, most of them hardly worn. There's even one still in its packet, pins and all. The one that your sister gave you last Christmas!' She eyed him sternly.

'You know I don't like shirts straight from the wrapping,' he grumbled. 'They're stiff and they itch!'

'I'll wash it specially.' She didn't flinch. 'Then you

can wear it this Sunday to chapel, all right?'

Mandy held her breath. She had the good sense not to interfere in this argument, even though the little wailing sound from inside the basket was tugging at her heartstrings. James still stood sentry by the door, ready to scarper.

Mr Williams pointed an accusing finger at the basket. 'My best blue shirt! My favourite!' he reminded her angrily. But it was the last squib of resistance. He knew when he was beaten.

'Now, Eric, it won't come to any harm. This young girl knows all about animals, don't you?'

Mandy nodded and gasped. 'My mum and dad are both vets. In Welford, at Animal Ark!'

Mrs Williams nodded too. 'See, she's a good girl. She's promising to come in here twice a day to help look after those poor wee things. They won't get under your feet. They'll just stay in there nice and cosy while Walton tends them.'

'Walton?' Mr Williams interrupted, looking curiously at Mandy.

'The mother cat,' Mrs Williams said, steady as ever.

'Daft name for a cat,' he grumbled, but he was definitely weakening.

'Well?' the fierce little woman demanded.

'Well . . .' He scratched his lined forehead with broad, workworn fingers.

'Right, that's settled then!' she said, like snapping a suitcase shut. 'The girl will come in here each day until the kittens can begin to fend for themselves.'

Mr Williams grunted.

'That means yes,' she reported to Mandy and James.

Mandy jumped up from the table, able to breathe at last. 'Oh, thank you!' she said in a rush. 'I'll go straight off and get some food and extra vitamins and things for Walton. I'll be back as soon as I can. Walton will need lots of looking after, being such a small cat, and we may have to help her feed her kittens. I'll bring milk and a dropper just in case. She won't have that much milk herself, and four is a lot for her to feed, especially being so run down when she was a stray! We'll need to— '

'Whoa, hold your horses!' Mr Williams backed off against the wall. 'Not so fast.' He turned to James. 'Now listen, lad, maybe I can talk sense to you!'

James stood to attention, ready to listen.

'Man to man, I'm telling you straight, mind. My wife Amy is too soft-hearted by far. Everyone knows that. And I've agreed to let those dratted kittens stay put on top of my shirts because of her. I don't like it, but I want a quiet life. And when my wife makes up her mind about something, I generally give in.'

Mrs Williams smiled at Mandy, her hands clasped meekly in front of her.

'But,' said Mr Williams, 'I just want to give your girlfriend here a word of warning.'

Mandy saw James's face colour up at the word 'girlfriend'. But Mr Williams thundered on.

'Now, I'm a mild-mannered chap, but before you both go running off for food and vitamins and whatever else, I want to make it clear that I won't put up with these smelly things camping out on my best shirts for a day longer than necessary, is that clear?'

James nodded. Mandy moved over to the door to stand beside him. They watched Mr Williams's face take on the old angry look. 'Quiet life or not, I'll give you just one week,' he warned. 'And that'll be your lot! After that, it's the end for the nasty little creatures!'

Mandy felt her heart go thump. She felt the blood drain from her face. 'What do you mean?'

'I mean what I say. I'm giving you seven days. Find good homes for those kittens within the week, or else!' He stood with his feet planted wide apart, his face like a storm.

'Or else what?' Mandy gasped.

'Or else I'll deal with them myself!' He turned and stamped out of the kitchen, slamming the door after him.

James and Mandy flew back home on their bikes, up and down the hills to Welford. At the back of her mind hammered the horrible phrase, 'deal with them myself'. Meaning what? Pictures of kittens drowning, hanging, being dumped in a sack by the side of a motorway flashed through her head.

She yelled goodbye to James at the Fox and Goose crossroads and pelted on up the track to Animal Ark. When she arrived, she threw down her bike in the backyard and rushed straight into the surgery.

'Mum!' she called. She dashed past Jean Knox in Reception, who was busy signing out Miss Martin's Yorkshire terrier, Snap.

Jean looked up and smiled. 'She's in the unit,' she said, but the door was already swinging shut.

'Mum!' Mandy slowed herself down and lowered her voice so as not to disturb the animals in their rows of cages and kennels.

'Hi, Mandy, over here!' Mrs Hope called. She had a blue-grey Persian cat up on the treatment table and was carefully feeling behind his left ear. She gave the cat a kindly stroke and popped him back in his basket. 'You're just about ready for home,' she promised. She turned to Mandy. 'Now, what's all the drama?'

Her mum stood there in her white coat. She wore her long red hair tied back as usual, but it was always escaping. With her big green eyes and friendly face, Mrs Hope had the knack of calming Mandy down. 'The school cat's had four kittens,' she reported.

'Ah!' Mrs Hope smiled. 'That explains the newspapers. Good bedding for a birth. Did you get there on time?'

'Yes, but she didn't like the place on the porch that we'd sorted out for her.' Mandy fiddled with the catch on the Persian's basket.

'No. They often don't.' Mrs Hope hooked her thumbs in her coat pockets. 'So?'

'So she gave birth in the caretaker's kitchen instead.'

'And?'

'And Mr Williams, the caretaker, hates cats!' Mandy looked at her mother with her wide blue eyes.

'Ah!' Mrs Hope settled back against the treatment table. Mr Hope came out of one of the treatment rooms to join them.

'Mu-um!' Mandy began to plead. 'He's given us a

week. We've got to find homes for four kittens in a week. Otherwise he's threatening to take them off somewhere and put them down!'

Mrs Hope looked at her husband. 'Hmm.'

'It's not fair!' Mandy exploded. 'He cares more about his stupid shirts than about the lives of four innocent animals! How can anyone be so mean?'

'Calm down, Mandy,' Mr Hope said. He was rubbing his beard thoughtfully. 'What's this about shirts?'

Mandy explained. 'Anyway, the kittens will be up and about in a few days, then it'll be OK to move them out of the stupid basket. Then he can have his rotten shirts back!'

'Mandy!' her mum warned. 'Don't be rude. Some people just don't like cats and you have to accept that.' She lifted the cat basket and began to head for Reception.

Mandy realised that her chance was slipping by. 'Mum,' she said, 'can I take some milk and some vitamins back over there tonight?' She knew from watching her parents at work in Animal Ark what help Walton would need to feed the kittens.

'Of course,' Mrs Hope nodded. She was already on her way out.

'And, Dad, can we take the kittens in here at the

end of the week? Please!' Mandy sidled up to him.

'Ah!' Mr Hope put an arm round her shoulder. He knew Mrs Hope was still listening. 'Now, Mandy, you know our rules about that.'

'I know, Dad, but this is different!' Mr Williams was going to kill the poor little things if she couldn't find them homes!

'We don't take in strays, you know that. We're not a charity, remember. We're vets.' Mandy guessed that it was a rule he might have bent a little. But his wife had a very firm business head. She came back towards them.

'The answer's got to be no, Mandy.' Mrs Hope was kind but firm. She put the cat basket down and spoke gently. 'Listen, the caretaker has already done you a favour and given you a week, hasn't he?'

Mandy hung her head and nodded miserably. 'It would only be for a while, Mum. We'd only have to have them for a while until Walton's finished feeding.'

'Then what, eh?' Mrs Hope glanced at her husband to check. 'That's right, isn't it, Adam? We can't suddenly change our rule about strays. We'd be overrun with them in no time. You've got to understand that, Mandy.'

Mandy nodded again. Her mum was always right,

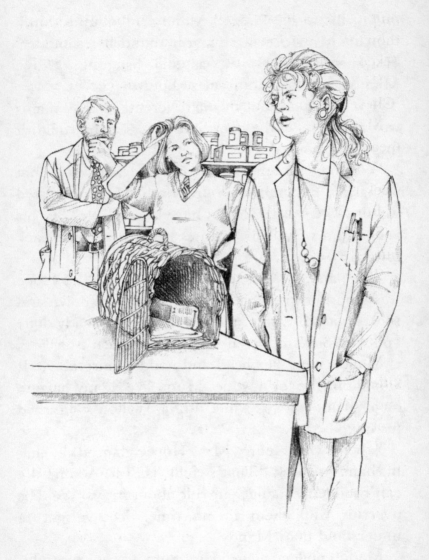

but it hurt a lot to agree with her sometimes. She thought of the four helpless kittens being carefully licked clean by a proud Walton.

'Now, listen,' Mr Hope said in his cheerful voice. 'Cheer up, this is a challenge!'

Mandy sniffed and looked up. 'How do you mean?'

'You've got a whole week; look at it that way! One week to find four good homes for four furry bundles of fun. You can do it!'

She looked up at his lopsided, cheerful grin. 'I can,' she agreed. 'Or rather, *we* can!'

'We?' her mum asked.

'Me and James.'

'You and James!' her mum echoed, raising her eyebrows. 'Well, then!'

Mandy ignored her. 'Yes! Four homes for four kittens!' Mandy began packing sterilised droppers and vitamin drops into her pockets. 'Easy. No problem!'

'Good girl,' Mrs Hope said, satisfied.

Mr Hope winked at his daughter. 'That's my girl!'

Mandy was dashing about, back to normal. 'I'll sort this out, just you wait!' She was out through Reception, grinning at Jean, stroking two black Labradors and a hamster, jumping on her bike and pedalling up the drive before her parents had time to draw breath.

Back at school, Mrs Williams opened the kitchen door to her and watched as Mandy gently lifted the lid of the laundry basket.

'Hello, Walton,' Mandy coaxed. Inside the basket it was warm and dark. The cat purred up at her. 'Come on, come and have some food!' She picked up the warm, soft cat and cradled her. The four kittens wailed miserably. 'Sorry, but mother cats need looking after too!' Mandy said as she closed the lid.

'There!' Mandy said as she set out milk and food on the kitchen floor for Walton. The cat arched her black and white back and rubbed against Mandy's legs. Then she settled quickly and daintily to her supper.

'Come and look!' Mandy whispered to Mrs Williams. 'Walton won't mind.' Walton raised her head briefly as Mandy lifted the basket lid once more, then carried on lapping milk. They peered together into the dark nest. Clean and dry, the four kittens nestled on Mr Williams's best blue shirt; blind and helpless, but quiet now, and snuggled against one another.

'Oh, my!' Mrs Williams shook her head. 'They look like drowned rats!'

'No, they don't. They're beautiful!' Mandy whispered. 'Look!'

'Well, at any rate they all look the same to me, all grey and furry and curled up like that.'

'No, they don't. They're very different; can't you see?' And Mandy promptly decided to give them names. She picked them up, one at a time. 'This one's Smoky, and this one's Patch.' She looked carefully at the two remaining kittens, then grinned. 'And this one's Amy. And this one's Eric!'

'Oh!' Mrs Williams stood back, slightly shocked, then pleased in spite of herself. 'Are you sure? I mean, I don't know what my husband will say!' She tut-tutted and smoothed her apron.

Mandy smiled and stood up as Walton finished her meal.

The cat leapt up on to the basket, back on duty. She sprang down into the dark well, ready to let the kittens suckle. 'I think we'll let her manage for now.' She put the lid back on, testing it to make sure the cat could push it off easily by herself. 'Maybe tomorrow we'll start giving the kittens extra.'

'Hmm.' Mrs Williams nodded. 'What time will you be back in the morning then?'

'About eight o'clock. Before school starts.'

The caretaker's wife showed her out. 'Mind you don't forget!'

'No way!' Mandy waved, picked up her bike and set off for home.

The sun was setting over the moor as she rode up out of Walton, past the new bungalows out on to the open road. The sky was pure red, the horizon dark brown. Mandy felt the wind. She was pleased with the day, happy that Walton had had such a good birth. She'd be a wonderful mother, even though she was so young herself.

Then Mandy's heart jolted. Smoky and Patch, Amy and Eric were all snuggled up for the night. There was a new world waiting outside for them, a big and dangerous place. Just now they were asleep. But Mandy tensed against the handlebars as she took the final curve down the hill into Welford. Her face frowned. She had a week to find four homes. Mr Williams's threat lurched out of the lengthening shadows like a giant from a fairy tale. 'Find good homes for them kittens within the week. Or else I'll deal with them myself!' he roared. Mandy knew he wouldn't relent. He meant what he said. A death sentence hung over the poor little kittens, and only she could save them!

Three

Mr Hope glanced up from the television as Mandy wandered in. The sitting-room was low, with wooden beams, a big stone inglenook fireplace and cosy red-patterned carpets on the old stone floor. It was a cold evening and a log fire crackled. 'Got any homework?' he asked.

'I've already done it.' Mandy flicked through a copy of *The Dalesman*. She was frowning and restless.

Mr Hope looked at her again. 'Why not take that back to your gran's?' he suggested.

Mandy nodded. She was thinking, thinking; what to do to find homes for those kittens? But she picked up the little magazine and drifted off down the hallway.

'Where are you off to?' her mum asked as she came in through the front door. She'd just got back from her yoga class, relaxed and smiling as usual.

'I have to clean out the rabbit hutch, then I'm off to Gran and Grandad's,' Mandy said absent-mindedly. She waved the magazine, still deep in thought.

'Say hello from me!' Mrs Hope shouted, but she got no answer.

Mandy let Flopsy, Mopsy and Cottontail out into the run in the back garden while she cleaned out their hutch and laid down fresh straw. Satisfied that their water was clean and that they were safely bedded down for the night, she set off up the lane to her grandparents' cottage.

In the cool evening light the mass of white lilacs in her grandad's garden gave off a strong, sweet scent. Even at this late hour he would be out in his greenhouse, pottering. 'Hi, Grandad!' she said with a wave. She stood to wait for him by the new camper van sitting proudly in their side drive.

'Hello, love!' His face lit up and he came out to greet her. He slid the greenhouse door closed. 'Come in, come in. Your grandma's inside writing letters.'

He showed her in through the kitchen into the cosy back room. The lamps cast a yellow glow and the flowered curtains were closed. 'Hello!' Mandy's grandmother shone her a wide smile. 'Guess what I'm doing.'

Mandy sat down opposite her at the table. 'Writing a letter!' She loved visiting her grandparents. Even when she felt down, like now, somehow they cheered her up.

'Not just any old letter!' her grandmother announced. 'This one is special. This one is to the Prime Minister!'

'Oh!' Mandy tried not to sound too surprised. She was used to her gran knitting impossible cardigan patterns and making kilos of rhubarb and ginger jam, not writing letters to prime ministers. 'What is it about?' she asked.

'It's about our post office. There's nasty rumours in the village that they want to close it down. Mr McFarlane told me about it when I went in to collect our pension earlier today.'

'Why do they want to close it?' Mandy couldn't imagine life in Welford without McFarlane's post office. She'd bought sherbet in there ever since she was tiny; she'd bought water-pistols, bubble-gum, comics, and sometimes soap powder for her mum when they ran out. When she'd forgotten James's birthday last month, she'd popped down to McFarlane's for a flowered card with a terrible verse:

Here's a birthday treat
For someone very sweet.
Kind thoughts and wishes too
For a friend as nice as you!

Gran raised her glasses on to her forehead. 'They say it's too dear to run. Too dear, I ask you! Honestly, they don't know what they're talking about! We have to stop them!'

'So Dorothy's writing to the Prime Minister. Always go to the top is what I say,' Mandy's grandad said. 'On her best notepaper of course!' He winked and handed her a glass of homemade lemonade.

'On my official notepaper. I'm writing as chairperson of Welford Women's Institute!'

Mandy looked impressed. Even the Prime Minister would have to listen to her grandmother when she was on her high horse. 'They won't close the post office,' she said. 'Not after they've read your letter!'

They all chuckled. 'You've spoilt my flow,' her grandmother said. She put pen and paper to one side.

She looked at Mandy's fidgety hands. 'Anyway, you've got something on your mind, I can tell.'

Mandy didn't need a second invitation. The story of Walton and her kittens poured out; how she was the school cat, but Mandy felt she must take charge. How Mr Williams had no heart at all. How she, Mandy, had to find homes for the kittens. Her grandparents nodded, tutted and nodded in all the right places. Mandy paused at the critical point and took a deep breath. 'Gran,' she said, trying to sound very reasonable, 'I've been thinking.'

'Yes?' Her grandmother gave her a sideways look.

'Well, I've been thinking that a cat would be the perfect thing for you here in the cottage. I mean, it's a bit lonely this far up the lane and you hardly see any neighbours, and a cat is really good company for . . .' She faltered and blushed.

'For old people?' Her grandad finished the sentence. He grinned. He was sixty-five; a gardener, a walker, a cyclist. He was fit as a fiddle.

'Yes,' she admitted. 'Anyway, they're lovely clean animals, and you don't have to fuss them. They look after themselves, and—'

'Whoa!' her grandad said. 'Steady on!' He looked helplessly at his wife.

'Look, love,' her grandmother spoke gently. 'It's a

good idea, and it's very good of you to be thinking of us like this, it really is. You're our beautiful, warm-hearted girl, you know that!'

Mandy saw a great big 'But' looming on the horizon. 'Yes?' she said, feeling her heart sink.

Her grandad took over. 'But we've just bought our smart new van. You know, our retirement treat!' He jerked his head sideways. 'There she stands in the drive all shiny and new, waiting to take us to the Italian Alps, to Provence, to Portugal!'

'To Scarborough, the day after tomorrow!' her grandmother put in.

Mandy nodded. 'So?'

'So we won't be at home to look after a pet as much as we were when your grandad was working. We'll be out on the open road, the autobahn, the freeway, with the wind in our hair and the sun on our faces!'

Mandy was shocked. She wondered if she'd ever see her grandparents again!

'Not all the time,' her grandad corrected. 'I still need to keep an eye on my tomatoes!'

'But too much of the time to be able to take in one of your stray kittens,' her grandmother said finally.

And Mandy had to accept that. Smoky was the one she'd been planning for them to have, with his cheeky face and his way of pushing the other three kittens out of the way when they were feeding. Now Smoky wouldn't be sunning himself on her grandad's patio after all. Mandy tried to swallow her disappointment.

'But . . .' her grandmother said, sweeping stray hair up into the pleat at the back of her head, 'we can still help!'

'How?' Mandy leapt at the promise. Her eyes lit up.

'We'll help you look for homes. How many kittens are there? Four?' Gran got on her thinking-cap. 'There's Eileen Davy at the Old School House, but she's on the main road, and she's already lost two cats to the traffic, poor things. There's Myra Hugill, but she has to look after her sick sister in York at present. There's Dora Janeki from Syke Farm, but she's a batty old thing and her new husband isn't known as an animal lover!'

Mandy seized each name, then let it drop as her grandmother counted them off on her fingers. She was beginning to feel hopeless again.

'Wait!' her grandad said. 'I've just had a brilliant idea!'

Mandy swung round to face him. 'What?'

'The post office!' he said, raising a finger.

Mandy looked puzzled. 'Not the post office just

now, Grandad. We're talking about Walton's kittens!'

'I know. That's why I mentioned McFarlane's. That's my brilliant idea!'

'Oh, I see!' her grandmother said. 'Yes, Tom, of course!'

'What? What?' Mandy didn't see at all.

'The notice-board in the post office! That's what we need!' Her grandad took a postcard out of the bureau and uncapped his old fountain pen. 'Watch.'

He wrote in beautiful copperplate letters:

WANTED!
FOUR GOOD HOMES
Cat lovers needed to provide
homes for kittens.
Please ring Welford 703267

'There!' he said, standing back and looking at his work of art. 'You can take it down to McFarlane's first thing in the morning!'

Mandy took the card. She nodded and smiled. 'Brilliant, Grandad!'

He screwed the top back on his pen. 'It's nothing, my dear,' he said modestly.

'Yes, it is, it's brilliant! We'll get millions of calls, you'll see!' Welford was full of animal lovers, and this was the perfect way to find them. Everyone went into the post office at some time during each day. Mandy hugged both her grandparents.

'Maybe not millions,' her grandmother advised.

'All right, dozens!' Mandy said, laughing at her own habit of exaggerating. They all laughed together.

She left the house, smiling and happy. She closed the gate with its Lilac Cottage sign, waved and set off down the lane. Tomorrow was Friday. She'd be down at McFarlane's with the lark, before the paper van or the milk delivery. She'd spend the weekend coping with all the phone calls. She ran home full of plans and preparations.

Mandy had arranged to meet James again to go into school early. She'd already been into the post office and pinned up her 'Wanted' card in pride of place on McFarlane's board. She greeted him cheerfully with, 'You're seven minutes late, James Hunter!'

James pushed his glasses back on to the bridge of his nose. 'Sorry,' he said. He screeched to a halt on his bike. 'I had to walk Blackie. Dad's away. And then I had to feed Benji.'

'Oh, well, then,' Mandy forgave him. Being late because of a dog and a cat was quite understandable. 'Let's go!'

They made up some time on the journey. Traffic was still light and they knew all the back ways. By five past eight they were knocking on the Williamses' kitchen door.

Mrs Williams opened it with a worried face. 'I thought you weren't coming! Come in, come in,' she said.

'Is something wrong?' Mandy was unpacking cat food and a carton of milk on to the kitchen table.

'I'm not sure. It's too quiet in there for my liking. Not like yesterday with all the racket. Even Eric noticed.' Mrs Williams watched anxiously.

Mandy lifted the basket lid. 'Hello, Walton!' she said. But the cat lay on her side and only managed a feeble miaow. 'Leave me in peace,' she seemed to say. She raised her head, but she didn't stretch and make her way out into the daylight to sort out some breakfast.

'Poor thing, she's exhausted!' Mandy said. 'James, you'd better open that can of food. I'll fetch her out.' She reached in, tenderly lifting out the tired cat. 'She'll be all right in a bit,' she told Mrs Williams. She knew from helping out at home that there was nothing seriously wrong. 'She just needs looking after.' And she set her down to feed.

Walton wobbled, steadied and settled eagerly to the dish of meat.

'What about the kittens?' James said.

Mandy cast an expert eye over the four huddled shapes. 'Fine!' she said. 'But we'll have to feed them. We'll need the droppers. And we'll have to use the ordinary carton milk for now.' She'd seen her mum and dad do it often enough. Now she hoped she could manage it all by herself.

James fetched the droppers from her bag. Mandy gently heated the milk. Then she lifted one of the feather-light bundles. She sat with it on her lap and eased open its tiny mouth. 'Come on, Patch, come on!' she coaxed.

She squeezed the rubber bulb of the dropper and took in milk from the warm pan. Then, while she held open the kitten's mouth with two fingers, she eased the glass tube between its lips with the other hand. She squeezed again and watched Patch's tiny tongue lick and then swallow the liquid. 'See?' she said to James. 'Now you have a go.'

He nodded and took another kitten, Smoky, out of the basket. Afraid but determined, he copied Mandy's actions with a second dropper. Smoky looked surprised, then gulped. James looked up in triumph.

'Well done!' Mandy said.

It was fifteen minutes later and they were just finishing with the last two kittens when Mr Williams tramped back in from unlocking the school. James and Mandy were busy stroking the kittens' throats to encourage them to swallow. Mr Williams heard the tiny mewing from the basket. 'What's up with the mother cat then?' he barked.

'Tired out,' Mrs Williams said. 'And you would be too.' She hovered by the sink like a worried relative.

'Hmm.' He turned back out of his kitchen, grumbling.

'This place is being turned into a cat hospital! A man can't even call his home his own any more!'

Mandy and James finished the feeding and cleared up the room to perfection. Walton was sitting on the step, taking the morning sun. She gave herself a thorough licking. Mandy bent to stroke her. 'Good girl,' she said. She was relieved when Walton decided it was time to return to her kittens. They watched her walk across the shiny tiles, jump up and nimbly lift the basket lid with one paw. Then she disappeared from sight.

'Clever thing!' James said. He looked at his watch. 'It's a quarter to nine,' he reminded Mandy.

They said a hurried goodbye to Mrs Williams and ran out through the garden and across the playground. A strong wind blew white blossom petals diagonally across the tarmac. 'What do you think?' James asked, pausing before they passed under the great stone arch of the main entrance.

'Oh, Walton will be all right,' Mandy said. 'She'll just have to take things easy.' She hitched her schoolbag higher on to her shoulder and brushed cat hairs off her navy blue skirt. 'But I'm not so sure about the kittens now.'

Mandy didn't want to scare James, but she thought the cat's milk might dry up. This sometimes happened when the mother wasn't strong. If so, the tiny things would soon starve to death. 'We'll have to wait and see. Perhaps Walton will be able to go on feeding them herself.'

'What if she can't?' James wanted to know.

Mandy thought of the kittens with their gradually opening eyes, their fluffier coats, their attempts to struggle up on to all fours. They still tumbled and collapsed like rag-dolls. She could hold them easily in the palm of her hand. 'Well, we'll just have to carry on feeding them ourselves,' she said.

All morning long Mandy had kitten worries on her mind. There was the old one of finding four good homes in less than a week, and the new one which she wouldn't confess even to James. But the question kept crowding in on her. It wouldn't go away. Walton was exhausted from the birth. The kittens were clinging on to life by a thread. And the question still whirled in her head as Mandy sat and ate her packed lunch in B Hall with Kate and Melanie: would they need to find homes for the kittens after all? Would the poor little things even survive?

Four

Mandy decided that the best answer to her question was a great big 'yes'!

You have to think 'yes' all the time, or life will get you down, she told herself. She and James would hand-rear the kittens if necessary. So she set about finding homes for them with even more energy than before.

She and James fed Walton and the little gang of kittens straight after school, then they cycled back to Animal Ark. 'We're going to make more notices!' Mandy announced. She led James upstairs and scrabbled under her bed, looking for some luminous pink card she'd stored there before Christmas. 'Then we'll be sure that every single person in Welford will read one!'

She liked to work in her room; it was an art gallery of animal posters. Horses and rabbits, dogs and cats stared down from her walls. Hardly a centimetre of wallpaper showed through, just how Mandy liked it. Mandy and James knelt on the floor to cut small rectangles of pink card. They chose broad black felt-tips and began designing their own ads. 'Where will we stick these?' James wanted to know.

'Shh, I'm thinking!' Mandy said. She wanted eye-catching words to draw people's attention. Finally she wrote in big capital letters:

KITTENS IN THE KITCHEN
Bring love into your life.
Cats make cosy companions.
Adopt a kitten. Ring Welford 703267.

It was catchier than her grandad's notice. She was pleased as she knelt back to judge the effect, while James finished his much more practical card:

HOMES NEEDED FOR FOUR KITTENS!
Remember, pets are for life!
If interested, ring Welford 703267

*   *   *

'I could put this one on your board in reception,' he suggested.

Mandy nodded. 'Good idea. Let's go down and ask Jean before she finishes for the day.' She knew Jean liked to know exactly what went up on the notice-board in reception.

They went downstairs and through into Animal Ark. Jean had closed the appointment book and was searching for her car keys. She had been their receptionist for five years and she was always losing her keys. Mandy knew all the places they were likely to be. She set about helping Jean search.

'Here they are!' Mandy lifted the blue book and handed the keys to Jean.

'Oh, silly me!' Jean said, as she always did. She wore her glasses on a silver chain round her neck and still managed to forget where she'd put them.

James tried not to smile. 'Can we put a "Homes Wanted" notice on your board, please?' he said.

Jean took the card, looked for her glasses, found them hanging down her chest and read the words. 'That looks fine. Just find a space over there beside all the others,' she said.

'Others?' James looked at Mandy. They scrambled across to the board. In the bottom corner there were at least six other 'Homes Wanted' cards. James and Mandy's faces fell a little.

'Only three of them are for kittens,' James said. Two others were for puppies, one for a pony.

Mandy counted up quickly. 'Yes, but that's fourteen kittens needing homes altogether!' Fourteen kittens in a tiny place the size of Welford.

'Come on, chop-chop!' Jean said. She was busy locking cupboards, windows, drawers and anything else that stood still. 'I want to shut up shop!'

They looked again at the notices, trying not to feel downhearted. 'Ours is the brightest card!' James said. 'And it's in the best position!'

Mandy agreed. 'I've had another idea!'

With the second bright pink card in her hand they shot off ahead of Jean, up the drive and down into the village. 'It's Friday. Gran will be playing badminton!' They cycled on past the post office, towards the village hall.

'So?' James overtook Mandy. His football training was coming in handy for stamina. They made for the hall, which was set back from the road, next to the church.

'They've got a Women's Institute notice-board in the entrance,' Mandy reminded him.

'Right.' James nodded and kept up the pace. Lots

of kind-hearted ladies came to the village hall to do flower arranging and cake icing, besides the Friday evening badminton club. It was a great position for one of their cards.

They almost bumped into Miss Davy from the Old School House as she came out of the hall, racquet in hand and not a silver-blue hair out of place. She turned and called in a shrill voice, 'Dorothy, one granddaughter!' She smiled at them and continued on her way.

Gran emerged, red-faced and breathless. She wore a bright turquoise tracksuit. 'Mandy!' She gave her a quick peck on the cheek. 'How nice. But it's thirteen-eleven, final game. I can only spare a second!'

'Sorry, Gran.' Mandy held up her KITTENS IN THE KITCHEN card. 'Can we pin this on the notice-board?'

Mrs Hope squinted at it. 'Oh, the kittens? Yes, yes, of course. Good idea. 'Bye, love!' And she dashed back to finish her game.

Mandy opened the glass door of the notice-board and made space between lists of flower rotas for the church, Brownie parades and a whist drive. She pinned her notice firmly in the centre, closed the door, stood back and admired it.

'Better!' James said.

They were pleased with the evening's work as they finally said goodbye and headed home.

After supper Mr Hope took Mandy into Animal Ark with a secret smile on his face. 'Come and see a new admission,' he invited.

Near the door of the residential unit was one of the see-through cages, shaped like a cat basket but made of clear plastic. Mr Hope picked it up.

'What is it?' Mandy could see the usual newspaper nest and a roll of soft grey rag, but she couldn't spot any animal in there.

'Squirrel!' Mr Hope said. A small black nose peeped out of the newspapers. 'A baby. Five weeks old.' Two large black eyes appeared, and out it came, the size of a hamster, with a long, long tail. Mr Hope unlatched the cage door and lifted it out. He handed the little grey squirrel to Mandy.

'Oh!' she said. She was speechless with delight. She felt its sharp little feet. She stroked its soft grey back while the baby tried to suck the end of her finger. 'Where's its mother?' she asked.

'She got run over.'

Mandy gasped, and her face crumpled.

'Yes, I know,' he said, looking at her. 'And this

little one would have died if someone hadn't found
him.'

Mandy shook her head. Life could be so cruel.

'You'll never guess who brought him in.'

'Who?'

'Old Ernie Bell from the cottages behind the Fox
and Goose.'

Mandy looked surprised. She knew Ernie Bell as a
grumpy, silent old man who shuffled down the village
street with his bag of shopping.

'He came in and handed him over. '''Ere,
veterinary,'' he says to poor Jean, ''just check 'im
over while I fix up a run for 'im in my backyard. I'll
be back for 'im in twenty-four hours. Just check 'e's
all right!'' And he leaves the little chap with Jean and
stomps off to build a wire netting run. Who'd have
believed it?' Ernie didn't have the reputation of being
soft on animals. Mr Hope put the baby back in its
cage.

'What's the roll of cloth for, Dad?' Mandy bent
down to study the squirrel in his cage.

'For comfort; something for him to snuggle up to.
Animals need a mother substitute, you know.
Something to take the dead mother's place.' His
voice was warm. He put an arm round Mandy.

'What are you feeding him with?'

'This stuff. It's the bottle food we give to orphan kittens. Why?'

Mandy was making new plans for Walton's brood. She took the box of white powder and read the list of contents and instructions printed on the side. 'Can I buy some of this from this week's pocket money?' she asked.

'For your school kittens?' Mr Hope lifted three boxes down from the shelf. 'Go on, take them. You don't have to pay!'

Mandy smiled. 'Walton's a bit weak at the moment. We'll have to help her feed the kittens properly.'

'Well, this stuff is much better than cows' milk,' Mr Hope said, adding an extra box. 'Mix it with boiled water, and use these little bottles with rubber teats. The kittens can suck these properly. Everything's sterilised of course.'

'How often?' Mandy realised that there was a proper way to do this. The kittens' lives depended on it.

'Every couple of hours for the first week.'

Mandy gulped.

'Less if the mother cat can still give milk herself, during the night for instance.'

'I think she can. She's just a very small cat and

she's tired.' Mandy was still determined to think the best.

'Well, then, this stuff four times a day will do the trick. Breakfast, lunch, tea, supper.' He glanced at Mandy's serious face. 'You're going to be busy,' he said. 'Any luck with finding homes for them yet?'

'Not yet.' She bent thoughtfully to the level of the baby squirrel in the cage. 'Will Mr Bell have to let him go eventually, back into the wild?'

Her dad shook his head. 'He's not allowed to. It's against the law, I'm afraid. That's because he'd never survive out in the wild now. Poor little chap, it seems he'll have to make do with Ernie's backyard for the rest of his life!'

Mandy nodded.

'Don't worry, there are worse fates,' Mr Hope said.

'Oh, I know.' But Mandy was still in a serious mood as she cycled over to school with the special kitten food. True, like Ernie Bell and the little squirrel, she was giving the kittens a chance of life. But without homes, would it be a life worth living?

She cycled and prayed that the notices in the post office, Animal Ark and the village hall would work. She wondered too whether she could persuade Mr Williams to give them a bit more time. A week was so

short! She leaned her bike against the hedge and went
up the steps into the caretaker's kitchen.

Once Walton was happily feeding, Mandy showed
Mrs Williams the new arrangements for Smoky,
Patch, Amy and Eric. To her surprise, the
caretaker's wife actually offered to help. 'Don't tell
my husband!' She pressed her thin lips tightly
together. 'He wouldn't approve!' She took Amy out
of the basket and gingerly snuggled her up against
her flowered apron, complete with feeding bottle.
'Poor little scrap!' she murmured.

Mandy smiled. 'She's fine. Look, she's hungry!'

Mrs Williams sat happily while the kitten fed. 'You mustn't mind my Eric,' she confided. 'I know he must seem like a grumpy old nuisance to you, but he's not so bad really.'

'No.' Mandy tried to believe it. All she could think of were Mr Williams's big boots and his loud voice. Hands as big as shovels. Temper like a volcano.

'You must think he's a stubborn old mule.'

'No!' Mandy knew she didn't sound sincere.

'Yes!' Mrs Williams looked down into the kitten's face. 'Yes, you do. But he loves his garden!' She bent sideways towards Mandy. 'Do you know, he keeps a squeezy bottle full of water out there on the porch. If a cat comes anywhere near his roses looking as if it's going to dig, Eric's out with the bottle, shooting at it. You should hear him when he scores a direct hit!'

'One wet cat!' Mandy joined in the laughter. 'I was thinking he might give us a bit longer than a week,' she said. 'Even when we find homes for them, Walton will have to go on looking after them for quite a bit. The less we need to move them around the better.' She looked pleadingly at Mrs Williams. 'Maybe you could persuade him?'

'Hope by name, hopeful by nature!' Mrs Williams said. But she was shaking her head. 'No, I know Eric. He's made up his mind!'

'Can't you just try?' Mandy was busy tidying up bottles and saucers.

But this time Mrs Williams wouldn't bend. 'No, it's not fair to him. He won't come into his own kitchen as it is. I know, I know,' she interrupted Mandy's protest, 'it's not sensible. But Eric's not always a sensible man. Who is? I'll tell you something else. He has a lot of pain, bending and kneeling and suchlike. Arthritis. In the knees. Very painful.' She lowered her voice. 'To tell you the truth we don't mention it in case the school gets to hear. He's worried about his job!'

Mandy nodded. Suddenly Mr Williams seemed human after all. 'I'm sorry to hear that.'

'Well, don't say I told you,' Mrs Williams warned. They were standing out on the porch. Walton was perched on the rim of the laundry basket licking herself clean. 'He's out at his darts match this evening. It cheers him up.'

Mrs Williams stared up at the pebbled clouds. 'But Eric's a worried man. It's the job, the house, everything. And the pain, of course. I can't even get him to go to a doctor.' She glanced at Mandy. 'So, you see, I can't ask him to do any more, can I? He's done enough already.'

Mandy agreed and smiled sadly. She rode home

slowly. She understood more about Mr Williams's bad temper now, that was certain. But it didn't stop time passing. The sand was running steadily through the hour-glass. They had five days left!

Five

'Hello, Welford 703267?' a woman's voice asked.

'This is it!' Mandy yelped, then lowered her voice to speak into the phone. 'Yes, this is Welford 703267.' She held her breath. 'Who's speaking please?' She gave her mother a hopeful thumbs up sign.

'Hello?' The voice sounded shy and cautious. There was a long pause.

'Hello, this is Amanda Hope. Who's speaking, please?' Mandy made a face of pretend panic at her mum.

'Hello, I want Welford 703267.' The voice seemed

strange, and unused to the telephone.

'Can I help you, please?' Mandy said firmly. What was going on here? Her mum had paused over the washing-up and was trying to listen in.

'Did you put a notice in the post office?' the woman on the end of the phone asked. 'Are you the person with the kittens?'

'I am!' Mandy said with a grin. 'I take it you're looking for a kitten?' Mrs Hope winked and carried on with the breakfast things.

There was a long, crackly pause. 'My name is Miss Marjorie Spry. I live at The Riddings. Please come to see me at two o'clock precisely.'

Then the phone went dead.

'Well?' Mrs Hope said.

Relief swept over her as Mandy realised that their plan was beginning to work. It was only nine o'clock on Saturday morning, and they'd already got a response! 'Yes!' she yelled, nearly jumping for joy. 'I'm off to tell Grandad!'

'Mandy, what if there are any more phone calls?' Mrs Hope was drying her hands, following her out.

'Write down the numbers on that pad, will you, Mum? I'm so thrilled I can hardly wait!' She rushed up the lane without a jacket. It was drizzling but she didn't care.

Her grandparents were stacking tins of soup inside the tiny cupboard aboard their camper. 'Tomato, minestrone, cream of chicken!' Her gran handed them up to her grandad and ticked them off her list.

'Tin-opener?' Her grandfather popped his head out of the sliding door. He saw Mandy. 'Hello, love!'

'It's worked! It's worked!' she greeted them. 'Your brilliant card, Grandad, it's worked!'

He rubbed his hands. Mandy's grandparents both stood there in their twin Aran sweaters, the drizzle wetting their grey hair. 'Has it now? You've got a response then?'

'Of course she's got a response, haven't you, Mandy?' Gran put in. 'Come inside. We're all getting wet.'

'Who is it then?' her grandad asked as he put on the kettle. 'Anyone we know?'

'It's someone called Spy. No, Spry. That's it, Miss Marjorie Spry!'

Gran shut the kitchen door firmly and wiped her feet. Her head went on to one side. 'The Riddings, isn't it?'

'Yes, The Riddings. Why, what's the matter? Do you know her?'

Her grandmother straightened herself up and bustled with the cups and saucers. 'Yes. She lives at the big house out on the Walton Road. Set back from the road. You know, the big old house!'

'I know!' Mandy said. They passed it every day on the way to school. It was well away from the traffic, with a huge lawned garden. The perfect place for a cat to live! 'She wants me to go and see her there at two o'clock this afternoon.'

'Does she now?' her grandmother said. 'That'll be one for the record book!'

'Why? What do you mean?' Mandy was nearly bursting with impatience. 'I thought you'd be pleased!'

'We are, love,' her grandad soothed.

'They're not usually keen on visitors, that's all,' Gran explained. 'In fact, I believe the last person they had over their threshold was Mr Lovejoy, the old vicar before Mr Walters, and that must be over five years ago!'

'No!' Mandy couldn't believe it.

'Yes, when their father died the two sisters went into a sort of hibernation. It's true!' Gran insisted. 'Still, that won't make any difference to you, I don't expect. If Miss Marjorie Spry wants to see you about a kitten and she's asked you along, you go and see her.' She patted Mandy's hand. 'They're harmless. A bit peculiar, but harmless enough.'

'Anyway, it's best to check these places before you send these precious kittens off to their new homes,' her grandad agreed. 'You've got to see if they're the right sort of thing!'

Mandy nodded, but she refused to be put off her stride.

'Take someone along with you,' her grandad suggested. 'Just to be on the safe side.'

'James will come with me,' Mandy said. She lifted a cardboard box full of bread, cornflakes, milk and margarine. 'Where do you want me to put these?'

Together they finished packing for 'the great trial run', as her grandad called it. He meant their first expedition in their new camper. Finally they were ready.

'Map?' Grandad said, climbing into the driving seat.

'Map!' Gran produced it from the passenger shelf.

He turned on the windscreen wipers. 'Wellington boots? Storm capes? Sou'westers?'

Gran flipped the map at him. 'Ready?' she laughed. They waved to Mandy. 'To sunny Scarborough!' she cried.

Mandy watched them disappear into the drizzle. There were still four hours to go before the visit to The Riddings. She would ring James to arrange to meet him, then fill up the morning with little jobs at Animal Ark, and of course by cycling over to feed Walton and the kittens.

Two o'clock came at last. They arrived to find the front lawn of The Riddings spread out like a cricket pitch. James and Mandy decided to leave their bikes at the gate.

'I wonder who cuts this grass?' James said. It went in neat strips, light and dark. The edges were neatly clipped.

'I do!' An ancient man in corduroy trousers growled at them from behind a laurel hedge. He was bent almost double, probably from years and years of clipping the edges of huge lawns, Mandy guessed. 'Have you come about a kitten?' he growled again.

They nodded.

'Miss Marjorie warned me about it. "Geoffrey," she said, "show the girl up to the door!" So I'm following orders. This way!' He trudged ahead of them up the gravel drive.

The house was as big as a hotel, built of stone, with pointed towers at each corner and battlements along the roof. It was covered in ivy. Though they passed it every day, James and Mandy could truly say that they'd never really paid much attention to it before. It had arched windows, stone pillars and massive steps up to a wide front door. 'Like a setting for a horror film!' Mandy whispered nervously.

Just when they felt they needed him most, their guide left them. 'This is as far as I ever go. Ring three times,' he said. 'Nice and loud, mind. You might have to wait.' And he went off, bowed and grumbling, to shave the lawn.

They looked at each other, shrugged, then James rang the bell. Silence. He rang again. And again. Finally someone began rattling locks on the other side of the massive door. 'Wait!' a tiny voice ordered.

'What do you think we're doing?' James whispered to Mandy, trying not to laugh.

'Shh!' Mandy said. They had to be on their best behaviour.

But even Mandy couldn't stop her jaw from hanging wide when the door finally creaked open.

The hall was the size of a ballroom, all in pink marble, with dark wood panels and glass chandeliers. But it was dull with age, and grey with years of neglect. What had once been as splendid as a fairytale had now decayed.

'Yes?' A lady stood before them. Her stick-like arms and legs poked out from a moth-eaten cream silk dressing-gown. She peered at them like a bat in the light.

'Miss Spry?' Mandy said uncertainly. A loud voice would have knocked the old lady down flat, she was sure.

'Yes!' She blinked her watery grey eyes. A skinny hand clutched the neck of her dressing-gown. 'We don't see visitors!' she chattered.

Mandy's grandmother had been right. No one had stepped this way for years. Curtains were closed to keep out the daylight. A collection of old blue and white china ornaments cluttered the window-sills. Great piles of yellow newspapers were heaped on shelves. 'Miss Marjorie Spry?' Mandy repeated, her heart sinking as her eyes took in the mess.

'Joan! Joan!' the woman shrieked. She began to close the door in their faces, but it was big and heavy. They saw the figure of another thin little woman come hurrying downstairs.

'Come in, come in,' this second person ordered in a thin voice. She was beckoning to them, half running across the hall. 'They've come about the kitten, Joan. Now open the door at once!'

And there they stood, two ladies thin as sticks, wild-haired, in matching silk robes. They had the same sharp faces. They had movements which

mirrored each other, and voices which echoed and mocked. Identical twins! Miss Joan and Miss Marjorie Spry!

'We don't want visitors!' the first one, Miss Joan, repeated with a birdlike twitch of her head.

'Yes, we do. I invited them!' Miss Marjorie argued. 'I want a kitten for this dreadful old place. I want to bring some life in here!'

Miss Joan stared stubbornly, silently back at her sister. Her hand stayed poised to slam the door shut.

'I do, Joan! I'm tired of living in this old museum of a place. I want some life. We're not old yet; let's make a fresh start!' Miss Marjorie pleaded. 'Look, this girl is advertising kittens. So let her in!'

At last Miss Joan gave way. Fascinated, Mandy and James stepped inside. To them it seemed like actually stepping into the past, into a kind of prison. Miss Joan pushed the door closed after them. It shut with a dull, heavy click. 'What kittens?' Miss Joan challenged. She looked her sister in the face. 'Who told me anything about a kitten?'

'I told you!' Miss Marjorie snapped. 'An advert in the post office. Welford 703627!'

'But I don't like kittens!' Miss Joan protested. 'You know that!'

Mandy stood in the middle of their argument, her

heart sinking right into her shoes by now. Miss Joan would never give in over this. Anyway, who'd want to leave a kitten where it wasn't wanted one hundred per cent by everyone in the house? She looked at James and could tell that he thought the same. They both sighed.

They watched as Miss Marjorie grew more and more angry. 'How do you know you don't like kittens?' Her eyes seemed to spark. 'Have you had one? Have you ever owned a cat in your entire life? Have you? Have you?'

She turned to face Mandy and James, smouldering with rage. '*I* like cats! Joan likes cats, though she says she doesn't! She only says it to be awkward. Yes you do!' she snapped at her twin. 'She's just a spoilsport. It's because it's *my* idea to bring a kitten to The Riddings, to help bring the place back to life a bit. She says no to all my ideas!' She nearly cried with exasperation. The tiny twins stood face to face like featherweight boxers.

'Anyway, I'm the older twin!' Miss Marjorie said grandly. 'And I have decided. Don't listen to her!'

'Well, they're still very young at present,' Mandy began to explain. 'We're only trying to sort out suitable homes for them in the future, you see.' Still she couldn't settle those doubts about this being a good place to bring one of her precious kittens.

'Where is it?' The older twin began poking at Mandy and James as if Amy might be hidden in one of their pockets.

'She's still with her mother. We're just starting to look, as I said.'

'Not here? Not brought it with you?' Miss Marjorie said sharply.

'Ha, ha, ha!' Miss Joan sang out. She did a little dance of delight. 'Ha, ha, ha!'

Miss Marjorie's thin patience finally snapped. 'Quiet!' she bellowed. She picked up an old black umbrella from the stand and launched it like a javelin at her noisy sister. It missed by miles, but Miss Joan froze on the spot. Then she grabbed a newspaper from a shelf and rolled it up like a baseball bat. James and Mandy stood with their mouths open. Who would believe them?

'Joan!' Miss Marjorie warned.

'You threw something at me first!' Miss Joan retaliated.

'Get out!' Miss Marjorie cried. 'Get out, get out!'

James and Mandy didn't know if she meant them or her sister. Everything was chaos. Mandy was growing sure of just one thing, though: this was no place for tiny Amy.

She knew this once and for all when Miss Joan, in her mischief, raised her rolled newspaper and began to chase Miss Marjorie from the hall into the study, a room at the front of the house. In a panic to stop them injuring each other, Mandy and James scuttled after.

Mandy stopped short. The room was lined from ceiling to floor with old books. But on the many tables scattered about the room were glass cases, dozens of them. Inside the dusty cases, perched, poised and perfectly preserved, were . . . stuffed animals!

A heron stood on one leg, forever fishing. An otter bared his teeth at an invisible enemy. A wildcat stared warily out, as if he knew he was about to be made extinct in Britain. Mandy squealed. Both hands flew to her cheeks.

'Let's go!' James said. For once, he took the lead. He grabbed her hand and made a run for it, back through the littered hall. They didn't turn to see if they were being followed. They just ran.

'Hey, you two!' Miss Marjorie called.

But they covered the distance to the gate in record time, ignoring the grinning gardener as they fled. Outside the gate they paused for breath. 'Well?' James gasped.

'No good,' Mandy said, almost in tears. The door was closed, the ivy still smothered the walls. The house seemed empty and grim. It would be another five years before anyone dared to disturb it.

'I agree.' They were both too shocked to think straight.

It was only the routine of cycling over to look after things in the Williamses' kitchen that saved them. They fed the kittens and cycled home to news from Mandy's mum.

Mrs Hope smiled across the treatment table where she was giving Snap the terrier his final injection. 'A Mrs Parker Smythe has been on the phone,' she said. 'She says she's interested in one of the kittens!'

Six

Mandy was up in good time next day. She'd done her chores, been over to feed Walton, and was back before her mum had finished breakfast.

'I'll take you up to the Parker Smythes in the car, if you like,' Mrs Hope offered. 'The arrangement was for nine-thirty.' It was the only other phone call about the kittens since the Misses Spry disaster, so Mandy felt glad her mother was coming along to give moral support.

'It's way out of the village, up by the Beacon.' Mrs Hope opened the passenger door of their big four-wheel drive. 'Hop in,' she said. 'Do we have to call for James as well?'

'No. He came over earlier to feed the kittens, but he's got a football match today, and his mum told him to take Blackie on an extra long walk, so he can't come.'

'Do the Hunters still have that cat of theirs?' Mrs Hope fastened her seat belt.

'Benji? Yes, course. Why?'

'He's getting on a bit, that's all.'

They took the high road out of Welford. Soon a steep hill loomed ahead of them. On top there was a stone pillar, visible for miles around: the Beacon.

'I expect James is still recovering from yesterday?' Mrs Hope said, her eyes set firmly on the road ahead. She went rapidly down the gears.

Mandy nodded. 'We both are.' Mandy was brave, but even she was rattled by the Spry sisters. She reckoned she was the least squeamish person around; she'd watched operations on stomachs, intestines, legs and hearts. But she shuddered at the memory of the poor stuffed creatures in the library at The Riddings; glass-eyed, covered in dust.

'You have to remember it was the fashion a hundred years ago. Most people have thrown those glass cases full of birds and animals away by now. But don't blame the twins too much. Poor things.' Mrs

Hope spoke quietly. She pushed a stray strand of hair behind her ear.

'Yes,' Mandy agreed. 'Animals look so much better alive and out in the wild, not stuffed inside some rotten case!'

'I meant the sisters!' Her mum glanced across at her. The hill was beginning to flatten out now. They could see the Beacon just ahead. 'They don't mean anyone any harm.'

'What, those two horrible old things! Nobody ever goes near them and all they ever do is argue!'

'Exactly,' Mrs Hope said softly.

And Mandy had to sit and think about that one as they pulled up outside a high hawthorn hedge with double iron gates, electronically controlled. 'Beacon House' was written in big gold letters. And 'No Parking. Trespassers will be prosecuted.'

Mrs Hope put on the handbrake. 'Anyway, this looks more straightforward.' She spoke into a little security machine on the gatepost, then the gate opened, as if by magic.

Mandy turned and took in the long distance view of the valley; its odd-shaped patchwork fields, scattered hillside farms, the road and river running parallel along the bottom, and Welford's two main streets criss-crossing in the far distance.

Then she turned again and followed her mother up
the drive. They went on foot through a small bluebell
wood, up to the big white house.

'What's that?' Mandy whispered. She pointed to a
flat tarmac area the size of a tennis court, but marked
with large white circles. It wasn't a tennis court
anyway, because that was on the other side, to the
right of the house.

'Helicopter pad?' Mrs Hope suggested. She rang
the doorbell.

Mandy gulped. A very blonde, very smart woman
opened the door. She was dressed in white shirt and
trousers, with gold necklaces, rings, bracelets. A lot
of gold. Even her shoes had gold decorations sewn
on.

Mandy felt her mother give her a little shove
forward to speak. 'Mrs Parker Smythe?' she asked
nervously.

The woman nodded. Her blonde hair stayed put.
Not a highlighted strand moved. Her smile revealed
two rows of perfectly even, perfectly white teeth
between shiny pink lips. 'Come in!' she said, like you
heard it said in posh films, usually with 'darling' on
the end.

They went in and she closed the door. 'Come this
way!' she said, all teeth and lipstick, and gold bits

dangling. Through the white hall with Italian tiles and rugs, into the kitchen. 'You must be Mandy? You put the nice pink advert in the village hall? I was collecting Imogen from the Brownies and we saw your notice!' she gushed.

Mandy nodded. She was finding it hard to fit in a word. Anyway, the kitchen made her feel that being there in her jeans and T-shirt and talking out loud in her ordinary voice was a bit of a mistake. It wasn't a bit like the old pine table and quarry-tiled floor of her own kitchen. This had shiny blue glass bowls and white gadgets everywhere, and no food anywhere to be seen.

Mrs Parker Smythe didn't seem to notice Mandy's shyness. 'Imogen is my little girl. She's seven!' she said proudly, as if Imogen being seven was like winning the Olympic Games single-handed.

'And this is Ronald, my husband. He's in satellite television!'

A balding man walked in, nodded and walked out again. He wore the palest yellow V-necked sweater and fawn checked trousers.

'He's going to play golf,' Mrs Parker Smythe told them. She shared another confidence: 'With Jason Shaw! You know, Jason Shaw, the actor! They're very good friends, Ronald and Jason!'

Mandy risked a glance at her mother, but didn't dare ask, 'Jason who?' Her mother was looking steadily out of the window, trying not to smile.

'We first met Jason when he came to film here, you know,' Mrs Parker Smythe rattled on. 'For an episode of *The Swallows in Spring*, this time last year. They used our swimming-pool!'

Mandy gulped again. She couldn't help it. Maybe tough little Smoky would be the right kitten for the Parker Smythes. The rough and tumble one. He'd bring them down to earth.

'Yes, our swimming-pool was used as a set for the programme. It belongs to the right period for the series. So Jason and the crew came up. That's how we met!' Mrs Parker Smythe bubbled on. She seemed to have forgotten all about the reason for their visit.

'Did you want a kitten for your little girl?' Mandy managed to fit in at last. Mr Parker Smythe wandered in and out again, apparently looking for something.

'Yes, well we have so much space here.' Mrs Parker Smythe spread her arms and her jewellery jangled. 'And such a big garden! And of course we have security cameras out there, so there's no danger of the poor little mite getting lost or anything!'

Mandy noticed her mother's eyebrows shoot up a fraction of a centimetre.

'And when we're away at our house in Tuscany, we still have Mrs Bates, our housekeeper, to come in and look after the kitten, feed it and so on.' Mrs Parker Smythe looked at her gold watch. 'Would you please excuse me a moment?' She dashed off after her husband.

'I wonder what he's lost,' Mandy whispered.

'His helicopter?' her mum said. But no; they heard huge blades begin to whir out on the pad. Clearly it had been wheeled out from its hangar and prepared for take-off.

They grinned. Mandy felt more relaxed. 'What if Smoky doesn't fit in here because he's only a plain, ordinary moggie?'

'Let's meet the little girl first, before we make any decisions,' Mrs Hope said.

Mandy nodded. She had to admit, once again, the signs were not all that promising.

'Oh, good, you're still here!' Mrs Parker Smythe floated back in after a few minutes. 'Now you must come through. Come and meet Imogen!'

She led them out of the kitchen across a giant conservatory full of artificial palms and pink-flowered cane furniture. But this was only a link to the house's main attraction; its indoor heated pool. This opened up from the conservatory through wide double doors.

The poolside was dazzling white and the water was deep blue. There was a fountain at one end, and windows from ceiling to floor all down one side. And there in the water, swimming like a walrus with just its nose and whiskers out of the water, was Imogen Parker Smythe.

'Imogen!' her mother called, clapping her jewelled hands smartly.

Imogen ignored her.

'Imogen, we have visitors!' her mother called again.

No response. Imogen swam round and round the fountain at the deep end. Mandy was amazed by her rudeness. *I'd never get away with that!* she thought.

Mrs Parker Smythe sighed. 'Come along, we'd better go down.' She went along the poolside carrying an apricot coloured bathrobe and a towel for her daughter. Mandy and Mrs Hope followed.

'Imogen!' Mrs Parker Smythe said in a coaxing voice. She crouched beside the water. 'Now come along, darling. Come and talk to Mummy about a sweetie, itsy bitsy little kittie for Immikins!'

Mandy swallowed hard. She stuck both hands into her jeans pockets. *Yuk!* she thought. She just hoped no one could read her mind.

'Shan't!' Imogen retorted, swimming in smaller circles.

'Oh, come on, darling! Remember, we talked about a sweet little furry kittie for you just this morning at breakfast. Remember?'

'No!' Imogen spat out water like a whale.

'Immie!' Mrs Parker Smythe was getting wet. 'Now come along out of there immediately, or I'll call your daddy!'

With a great sigh and much splashing Imogen Parker Smythe heaved herself out of the water. She was a mousy-haired, slightly overweight little girl with a constant scowl. She squirmed as her mother wrapped her in the bathrobe. She pushed away the towel offered for her dripping hair. Instead, she shook her head from side to side like a dog.

'Hello,' Mandy said. She forced herself to take the lead in this conversation.

Imogen tossed her head and sniffed up great drips of water.

'I hear you want a kitten?' Mandy went on.

Sniff. Sniff.

'I've got four kittens. Four tiny ones just a few days old. But soon their mother will finish feeding them, and after that they'll need really good names

and somebody to look after them!' Mandy explained in what she thought was a clear, sensible way.

'I know that!' Imogen snorted. 'Everyone knows that!'

'Immie!' Mrs Parker Smythe chirped.

'They'll need good homes, and someone very kind and careful to look after them!' Mandy said in a much cooler voice.

'What colour are they?' Imogen demanded, eye to eye with Mandy. 'I want a white one!'

Mandy paused. 'Well, the colour isn't that important really, is it? I mean, a kitten isn't a kind of toy, is it? It's a real live animal, you know. Soon it'll grow into a big cat that will still need feeding and taking to the vet, and somewhere clean and airy to sleep. In fact, it will need lots of looking after!'

Imogen turned to her mother. 'I only want a white one!' she whined.

'But, Immikins!' Mrs Parker Smythe looked helplessly at Mandy.

'You said I could have a white one!' The child stamped her foot. 'A white kitten! A fluffy white one with long fur! I want one! I want one!'

Mandy was furious. She felt like stepping right up to the revolting girl and pushing her back into the swimming-pool. 'Kittens are not toys!' she repeated. 'And they don't have to match your colour scheme!'

'Mandy!' Mrs Hope warned under her breath.

But Imogen was equal to the fight. She took a long look at Mandy, then she screwed her face tight and whined loudly. 'O-o-oh, Mummy, make the horrible nasty girl go away! I don't like her! Make her go away, Mummy!'

Mrs Parker Smythe fell for it. 'There, there, Immikins, don't cry!' she said. She cuddled her daughter at a distance, so as to keep dry. 'You don't have to have a kittie if you don't want one, darling. There, there!'

Mandy saw Imogen's face peep out at her from behind podgy little fists. Imogen sneered up at her. 'That got you!' she seemed to be saying.

Mrs Hope was pulling at Mandy's arm. 'Time to go,' she urged.

But Mrs Parker Smythe had left off cuddling Imogen and came towards them. 'Take no notice,' she whispered. 'Imogen's in one of her moods. You can bring the kitten anyway. I'll talk her round.'

But Mandy stood her ground. She was deter-mined to have her say. 'Mrs Parker Smythe,' she announced, 'I'm afraid this would never work!'

Mrs Parker Smythe's gold jewellery trembled as she went back and bent over her daughter.

Mandy continued. 'To keep a pet you have to be a sensible, caring person. Animals have rights, you know, and one of those rights is to belong to a good, responsible owner!' She paused for breath, but there was no stopping her now. 'And I'm afraid Imogen just doesn't qualify! I couldn't imagine anyone *less* suited to look after Smoky, Patch, Amy or Eric!'

She glared down at them as they hugged each other by the side of their swanky pool. She turned on her heel. Her trainers squeaked on the wet tiles all the way down to the French doors, but she didn't care. She swung through the conservatory, the designer kitchen, the hall. Mrs Hope caught up with her halfway down the drive.

'Sorry, Mum,' Mandy said, for being rude. But her mother didn't seem to mind as they marched out to the car, shoulder to shoulder.

'No good,' Mrs Hope sighed and opened the door.

Mandy sank back in the passenger seat. She felt bitter about spoilt little rich kids and their soft mothers. And she was panicking about the kittens. Two replies to their adverts so far, and two disastrous results! 'No, no good again!' she said.

Tears of disappointment threatened, but she bit

them back. She had to carry on looking. She had to succeed!

Seven

The weekend was almost over, and still the kittens were homeless. Mr Williams would kick them out of his kitchen on Thursday, or do something dreadful. For him, they weren't creatures with feelings. They were just nuisances to be got rid of.

'That's how some people think,' Mandy's dad explained. 'Especially some older people round here. You don't get soft on animals when you live on farms or in the villages. When Mr Williams was young, they drowned unwanted kittens in the rain barrel behind the barn. I don't suppose they even thought it was cruel.'

Mandy shuddered. As far as she was concerned, it was murder.

'Come on, help me take this young chap along to Ernie's!' Mr Hope suggested. He picked up the plastic cage containing the baby squirrel. 'I've checked him over and he's as right as rain. He can go into the run at the back of Ernie's house and we'll see how he gets on.'

They set off on foot, down their lane to the main street. It was a sunny afternoon, with blossom everywhere. Gardeners were out with their trowels and pruners, making the flowers stand to attention. 'Good afternoon,' people said pleasantly. Some stopped to look at the squirrel and pass the time of day.

Mandy liked the fact that everyone knew her father. He'd been born up at Lilac Cottage and had lived in Welford all his life, except for his college days in York. The older villagers still called him 'young Adam' or 'Tom Hope's lad'. They knew he was a brainy boy, he'd been to college, and he was known as a decent vet. At any rate, he was one of them.

The women came out of their houses and made a fuss of Mandy, while the men described problems with moles on their lawns, or a sheep stuck in the cattle grid at the back of the Janekis' farm. The squirrel scampered in its cage, accepting offers of peanuts through the grille.

At last Mandy and her father reached the Fox and Goose. 'It's only taken us an hour and a quarter!' she remarked.

Mr Hope laughed and went into the pub for half a pint of beer and a can of cold Coke for Mandy. They spent another fifteen minutes in the last rays of sunshine, sitting on a bench, gossiping.

'Right!' Mr Hope wiped his beard clean of any stray froth and stood up. He sounded purposeful at last. 'You bring the squirrel, Mandy.'

She followed him across the cobbled courtyard of the pub. The squirrel scuttled in its cage.

'That used to be the forge,' Mr Hope said. He pointed to the plush restaurant at the side of the pub.

'I know, Dad, you've told me!'

He carried on regardless. 'My own grandfather had the place in the 1920s.'

'I know, Dad!' Boy, was he embarrassing sometimes. Mandy shuffled from one foot to the other. Soon she'd have to cycle over to Walton for the regular evening feed. The kittens were doing well on the special liquid food, and Walton herself was looking sleeker. Mandy was pleased with their progress. 'Come on, Dad, let's go!'

He turned and grinned. 'Sorry, love!' And he led
the way again, down the side of the pub to a squashed
up row of tiny two storey stone cottages that had seen
better days. There were five cottages, all with beaten-
up doors, unruly ivy and great stone slabs making a
pathway along the length of the row. Most of the
front doors stood open in the sunshine.

'Now then, young Adam!' a gruff voice said.

Mandy and Mr Hope stopped at the first house.
She might have known they wouldn't make it to
Ernie's without at least two more interruptions.

'Hello, Walter. Lovely day!' Mr Hope stopped
and leaned in at Walter Pickard's door. 'How are
things?'

'Mustn't grumble,' the old man said. 'Now then,
young miss!'

Mandy smiled hello. Walter never remembered
the name of anyone under thirty. It was just 'young
miss' or 'young sir'. He was a retired butcher, a
Wednesday evening church bell-ringer alongside her
grandad, and, what's more, a cat lover! Two lovely
old ginger cats sunned themselves on his front
doorstep.

'What have we here?' Walter said, bending and
tapping the cage. Inside, the squirrel sat up and
begged. 'Hey up!' Walter said, half laughing. He

went off down the dark narrow hallway and came back with a piece of cream cracker which he fed to the squirrel.

Mandy liked Walter. He was a big man, but his deep voice was gentle, and his lined face under its flat cloth cap was always smiling. His wife had died last year, but Walter's three cats still kept him company. Mandy liked him because of his smile and his cats. What she couldn't understand was how he'd spent his entire working life in a butcher's shop. All those cold sides of beef hanging on their hooks. All those dead chickens. Mandy shuddered. She was glad she was a vegetarian. These days she hardly ever ate meat.

Mr Hope glanced at his watch. 'Do you know if Ernie's in?' he asked.

Walter nodded. 'Most likely.'

'In that case I'll just pop this little fellow along to him.' Mr Hope picked up the cage, saw Mandy was busy stroking the ginger cats and said, 'I'll leave you here, Mandy, to tell Walter the story of Ernie Bell and the orphan squirrel!' Then he wandered off down the row.

Mandy recounted the sad story of the squirrel.

'Ernie Bell!' Walter said, shaking his head. 'He's adopting a squirrel, that miserable old devil!' It was like saying he, Walter Pickard, had won the football pools.

Mandy had her hand deep in the soft warm fur of one of the old ginger cats when an idea struck her. She looked up from her cross-legged position on the path. 'Walter, how many cats have you got?' she asked casually. But the excitement of the idea was beginning to make her heart beat faster.

'Three,' he said. He sat down heavily on an old wooden stool just inside the doorway. 'That one's called Scraps because she feeds on any scraps I give her. She's not the least bit fussy.' He pointed to the one Mandy was stroking. 'And that's Missie over there, because she's a right little madam, and only eats the best fish and chicken breast.' This other ginger cat was contentedly purring in the sun. 'Then there's Tom. He's indoors at present.'

Mandy listened quietly, but she thought furiously,

'We used to have another one, mind,' Walter went on. 'My Mary loved cats, and it was her favourite, Susie, that passed away just after Christmas.' He sat with his own memories for a while, then pulled himself round. 'Susie was a dainty little cat, just like my Mary. That's why she was her favourite.' He smiled. 'Yes, indeed.'

Mandy nodded. She knew it was now or never.

'Why not get another?' she said. 'It just so happens I'm looking for homes for kittens right now, and there's one little dainty one, a little tortoiseshell called Amy, who'd be just right for you, I'm sure!'

Walter listened. He seemed to like the idea. 'A tortoiseshell?'

'Yes. They're only a few days old, and we're partly having to hand-rear them, James Hunter and me, because the mother's too weak. She was a stray. But we'll need homes for all of them. Good homes!' She stressed the 'good' and looked up at Walter.

He blew out his cheeks like a trumpeter. 'A tortoiseshell?' he repeated. Mandy pictured a young kitten scampering about on the warm flagstones all summer long, jumping up at his wallflowers, tumbling in over the step.

'A really lovely little tortoiseshell!' she insisted. She held her breath.

'Aye, I'd love one,' Walter sighed.

'Oh, it'd be a perfect home for Amy!' Mandy told him. 'It's nice and quiet back here, off the road, and the older cats would look after her, and you know all about kittens. It would be ideal!'

Say yes, she prayed. *Say yes!*

But a shadow crept down the hallway. A big, butch bruiser of a shadow padding up to the doorstep

in the sinister shape of Tom.

'Hello!' Mandy said to the barrel-shaped cat. He
stood four-square in his doorway. He bared his teeth
and hissed. 'Hello there!' She ran her fingers up and
down the flagstones. 'Here then!' she coaxed. He
ignored her game. Sulkily he padded across the step,
back and forth, strong shouldered, wide mouthed.
He was a black and white bully with a pirate's black
patch over his left eye, a chewed left ear and ragged
whiskers.

'Ah, Tom!' Walter said with a sigh of regret.

Tom arched his back at Mandy and spat. He
padded around the two ginger females, just checking
up on them. Then he stood and stared again at
Mandy.

'There's Tom to consider, you see,' Walter
explained. 'Scraps and Missie would be fine. But not

Tom.' The old man shook his head. 'Just take one look at him. He'd eat a new kitten for breakfast!'

Mandy could believe it. Never had she seen a cat like Tom; a heavyweight, a bouncer, a sumo wrestler of a cat!

'No,' Walter said sadly. 'Much as I'd like to, I'm afraid old Tom wouldn't be happy with a stranger about the place. You can see my problem?'

Mandy nodded. Though she was desperate, she had to agree.

'Never mind, Thomas, no one's going to come upsetting you.' Walter bent forward to scratch the chewed-up old ear. 'Just relax, old chap!'

The cat blinked and tilted its colossal head in victory. He'd staked out his territory and won.

Sadly Mandy got to her feet. Such a missed opportunity! But her dad was returning with the empty cage. 'Ready?' he asked.

They said their goodbyes to Walter and set off across the pub yard. The old man continued to sit on his stool, cats at his feet.

'I say,' Mr Hope said, glancing backwards, 'Old Walter's fond of cats. Why don't you—'

'It's all right, Dad,' Mandy interrupted, 'I already have. I asked him and he says he'd like another kitten, but Thomas the Terrible wouldn't appreciate

it.' She joked, but she was feeling very low. 'In the
end he said no.'

'Ah, well,' Mr Hope said, swinging the empty
cage, lost in his own thoughts.

All the gardeners had gone inside for tea, so their
walk home was much quieter and quicker. Mrs Hope
had prepared their own evening meal, knowing that
Mandy would want to cycle over to school before it
got dark. No one mentioned the kittens. If they had,
Mandy felt she might have broken down. And her
mum and dad knew when not to fuss. She ate, then
packed her bag. She met James at the post office, and
together they cycled to Walton.

Mr Williams was in a very bad mood.

'It's Sunday night,' Mrs Williams reminded them.
'He always gets like this on a Sunday night.'

He'd been stamping about the kitchen when they
arrived, but as soon as he saw them, he grunted, took
his Sunday newspaper and headed out of the room.

'It's because it's Monday tomorrow,' Mrs
Williams explained. 'W-O-R-K! The dreaded four-
letter word.'

Then Tuesday, then Wednesday, Mandy thought
with a lurch. She wanted to stop the clock, or at least
to stretch the days. The trouble was, as each visit to

the kittens came and went, she grew fonder of them. They were about twelve centimetres long and weighed just 100 grams or so. They hadn't yet struggled to their feet and their eyes were still closed. Smoky was strongest, but Patch gave him a good scrap in their fight for food, while Amy and Eric were patient, more content.

Now was the time to ask Mrs Williams if they could gently tip the laundry basket on to its side so the kittens could begin to sniff the daylight of their own accord. 'And then Walton might be ready to move them to a new nest,' Mandy suggested.

'What, tip it over and leave it there?' Mrs Williams asked. She looked doubtful. 'It'd make the place look a terrible mess!' But in the end she agreed. The basket could be tipped on to its side.

As James and Mandy fed each of the kittens in turn, Mr Williams stamped back in. He was wearing a very clean, very stiff white shirt and a maroon tie. He looked smart in his dark suit, but he walked awkwardly, Mandy noticed for the first time. He frowned at the upturned laundry basket.

Mrs Williams leapt to her feet. She was ready for chapel, in her fawn dress and silk scarf. 'Now, Eric!' she warned. She saw him glaring at the two kittens who happened to be pulling by mistake at the sleeve of his best blue shirt. They were seeking out Walton, but getting tangled in the shirt instead. 'It's only till Wednesday night!' she promised.

He didn't even grunt. He just stamped out on to the porch.

'Good job it's Sunday!' Mrs Williams whispered.

'Why?' James asked.

'Eric never swears on a Sunday,' she said. She raised her eyebrows. 'Otherwise the air in the kitchen would be blue as that shirt!' She sighed as she picked up her shiny brown handbag. She checked her keys. 'Drop the latch as you go,' she reminded them. Then she followed her husband down the road to chapel.

Mandy shook her head. The kittens were all safe for the night. James was washing Walton's feeding bowl and saucer, and the mother cat was coming to Mandy for a final grateful stroke before she settled down with her kittens. 'I wish . . .' Mandy said. But she never finished the sentence.

James felt helpless too as they checked the kitchen, turned off the light and locked the door. 'That's what I like about computers,' he said out of the blue as they pulled up out of town on their bikes.

'Huh?' Mandy said. 'What are you talking about?' James sometimes came out with these odd things.

'Computers. That's what I like about them. They're straightforward and simple, and they never make you feel bad.'

'Not like people and animals, you mean?'

He nodded. 'And you can just switch them on and off, no problem.'

They cycled for a while in silence.

'But they go wrong!' Mandy objected. You shouldn't prefer machines to live things, surely.

'So do animals,' he said. Another silence. 'Like Benji.'

'Oh, what's wrong with Benji?' Mandy asked. James had had Benji for as long as she could remember; he was a lovely, docile black tomcat.

'Dunno,' James said. 'My mum has to bring him into the Ark tomorrow morning to see if they can find out.'

Mandy nodded and sighed. 'Well, see you tomorrow, early?' she said by way of goodbye.

'Tomorrow early,' James promised, as they each rode their separate ways.

Eight

One little victory would be enough, Mandy thought. One home for one kitten. It wasn't asking much, and it would be a start. She went through the names they'd had so far, just to make sure that none of them would do.

Thinking hard, she passed Simon a thermometer to take the temperature of a Border collie who was just recovering from parvovirus. It was only because she was so young and strong that she'd survived.

Simon stroked the dog's long, black coat. 'At least they'll remember to have her vaccinated from now on,' he said.

Mandy nodded, but she was thinking of Miss Marjorie Spry. Surely even she could remember to open a tin of cat food each day. The kitten could be given a quiet, cosy corner in the garden shed if that old gardener would clear a space. Mandy stopped scooping meat into the dog bowls and stood, fork poised.

'A penny for them,' Simon said with a smile. He was looking at his watch.

'What?' Mandy was imagining Amy snugly tucked up behind the old flowerpots and garden shears.

'A penny for your thoughts!' Simon took the fork and carried on preparing bowls of food for their resident cocker spaniel and two black Labradors. 'You don't usually daydream on the job!' he said.

'Oh, sorry!' Mandy gave a sigh. Of course, The Riddings wasn't any good. Simon had broken her dream. She recalled the frozen snarl of the stuffed wildcat, the hopeful glass stare of the heron. All those dusty cases with dead animals in them. She feared it would never work to send Amy there, and the poor kitten was still homeless.

'Best get a move on,' Simon said. 'Here, you do the hamster dishes next, while I clean out the cages. And remember Flopsy and Co. out at the back!'

Mandy took the scoop full of rabbit food out into the back garden. There was always the Parker Smythe mansion for Smoky, she told herself. She knew she was clutching at straws, though. How long would it be before the kitten lost its novelty? Two days? Mandy sighed again. And that was only if Imogen would accept a grey cat. No, she wouldn't wish Imogen Parker Smythe on her worst enemy, let alone on precious Smoky.

If only Walter Pickard's old tomcat had been better tempered! Mandy stood there with a handful of oats and sunflower seed mixture, deep in thought.

When she went inside, Simon had finished the hamster cages. He took a last look at her, and in his quiet way took charge. 'Look,' he said, 'I'll finish here. I thought you had to get off to school early again.'

'What? Oh, yes, thanks!' Mandy dusted down her hands and scrambled out of her white coat. 'Is that the time? I must dash!'

She was out of Animal Ark and in her school uniform when she bumped into her mum on the stairs. 'Any phone calls?' she asked, hoping for more responses to the adverts.

'No,' Mrs Hope said.

'Right.' She hadn't really expected any this time. Her hopes were not high.

Then she was out of the house, up the lane to meet James outside McFarlane's. Her mind was still working overtime. *I suppose I could always try Walter again*, she thought as she screeched to a halt. James was already there.

'Sorry I'm late!' she said.

James was quieter than usual as they cycled over, but Mandy had a lot on her mind, too.

School went by in a semi-daze. She got two questions wrong in history, and a telling off from Mr Holmes. 'What's wrong, Amanda? This isn't like you. Been watching too much television, I expect. Now just pay attention, please!' Mandy went red and hot, and tried to concentrate.

She was thinking of the kittens when a group of friends asked her if she was going to the disco on Friday. Mandy didn't answer. 'Oh, be like that!' one said. They were all giggling about something or other. 'Don't think we care whether you come or not! You're not the centre of the universe, Mandy Hope!' And they flounced off.

Mandy shrugged. It was time to go and feed the kittens.

And she was still thinking of them when James

came up after school and told her quietly that he had to go straight home tonight. He'd promised his mum specially.

Mandy nodded. 'See you tomorrow then,' she said. She had a plan in her head; not much of a plan, but she'd decided she would visit Walter again. She'd feed the kittens first, then she'd call in at the cottages. Anyway, it couldn't do any harm. She'd invent an excuse; maybe she'd visit Ernie Bell's squirrel and just 'happen' to call in on Walter. He mustn't think she was pestering on purpose.

'Hello, young miss!' Walter greeted her from his open door. 'Where's that grandad of yours got to? I've not seen him round here lately.'

Mandy propped her bike against the end wall. 'Hi, Walter.' She tried to sound casual. 'He's off touring in his new van.' She gave him one of her cheeriest smiles. It was an effort, but she wanted to be bright and breezy.

'Camping!' Walter said with a low whistle. 'At their age!'

'Not exactly.' She explained the luxuries of the modern mobile home. 'It has a fridge, electricity, everything!'

'Hmph! Don't they have a fridge and electricity at their house, then?'

'Yes.'

'Well, then, what's the point?' Walter said. His ginger cats came padding elegantly down the hall.

Mandy gave in and changed the subject. She stroked Scraps and Missie. 'I've just popped by to see Mr Bell's squirrel,' she said casually. 'To see if he's settled in OK.'

Walter nodded. 'Aye, if he'll see you,' he said. 'Ernie doesn't always answer his door!'

'I'll be back in a minute,' she said.

She walked up the flagged path to the end of the row. She knocked hard. The green door was faded and flaking; it needed a good coat of paint. And it had an old lion knocker which hadn't been cleaned for years. It was stiff with disuse. She knocked again.

'Hold your horses, hold your horses!' Ernie grumbled from inside. She heard bolts sliding, locks turning. Finally, Ernie opened his front door.

Mandy heard Walter mumble and turn back inside his own house. She was left to face Ernie alone.

'Yes?' Ernie snapped. He was a small man with a shock of straight white hair rising back from his lined forehead. There was something birdlike about his sharp nose, his bright, dark eyes. He wore an old waistcoat and a shirt without a collar. 'Yes?' he said again, peering at Mandy.

She introduced herself as the vet's daughter. 'My dad brought back the squirrel yesterday. How is he?' she asked.

Ernie frowned. 'Fine, fine. What do you want now? You can't have him back, you know. I've paid the bill!'

'No, I don't want to take him back,' Mandy tried to explain.

'Good. It cost me a fortune just to have him checked over, I can tell you. But I paid!' he insisted. He stood there, frowning.

'No, I—' Mandy hesitated, then changed tactics. 'What's his name?' she asked.

Ernie paused. 'Sammy,' he said, as if he didn't want anyone to hear. 'All right?'

'Yes, it's a nice name. I was just wondering, could I take a look at him, please?'

She waited until Ernie made up his mind. He stared at her, thought a while, then nodded. 'This way,' he said at last.

He led her down a dark passage, through his kitchen and out into the backyard. Four gardens along the way, Walter was out in his garden. He leant his forearms against his fence top. 'Now then,

Ernie!' he greeted his unfriendly neighbour.

Ernie grunted. He stood by, watching suspiciously as Mandy inspected the squirrel run.

'Sammy!' Mandy called gently. There was a sturdy hutch at the far end of the run, with a small hole for an entrance, which only something as tiny and agile as a squirrel could use. The little creature poked out its round grey head.

'Here,' Ernie said. 'Tempt him with these!' He handed Mandy a few peanuts from his trouser pocket.

And Sammy bounded out of the hutch. He clung upside-down to the netting, swinging like a trapeze artist towards her. His feet never touched the ground.

Mandy held out the nuts in the palm of her hand. Delicately Sammy watched, reached out a paw and snatched the food. He swung away to a safe distance, then nibbled.

Mandy studied him. This was only the second time she'd been this close to a squirrel. The run was ten metres long, made of timber and fine mesh. Very safe. 'This is great!' she told Ernie, tapping the framework.

'Hmm.' Ernie nodded. 'So it should be.' He too was watching the squirrel, and his face had lost its

frown. 'I've had a fair bit of practice, mind you. I was a carpenter for more than fifty years!' Then as if he'd given away top secret information, his mouth clamped shut and the frown returned.

'Well, it's great,' Mandy said. 'Really sturdy and safe. I'm glad Sammy's found such a good home!' It was almost enough to take her mind off homeless kittens. But she could see Walter along there in his own yard, and she was desperate to talk with him. She remembered her real purpose: to persuade Walter and old Tom to change their minds. 'Can I come and visit Sammy again?' she asked Ernie.

He swallowed hard, but he nodded slowly. 'You can call again,' he agreed. 'It might not always suit me to answer the door, you understand. But you can always try.'

He followed her out to the front of the house. 'Well, Mr Bell!' Mandy was about to turn and thank him again for showing her the squirrel, but the flaky green door was already closed. And like a figure in a Swiss cuckoo clock, Walter was already out at his own front door. As usual, he was not minding his own business.

Mandy wandered towards him. She was going to ask, 'How's old Tom today?' and then gently add the idea that perhaps Tom would take to a new kitten, if they introduced him to the idea gradually.

But Walter must have been a mind-reader. She never got any further than 'How's old Tom?' before he cut her short.

'It's no good you wheedling away, young miss!' Walter laughed at her surprise. 'I know what you're going to ask, and Tom's answer is still no!'

As if to confirm this, Tom came bowling round the corner at top speed and bashed straight into Mandy's bike. Down it crashed. Tom wailed loudly, leapt the spinning wheels, and vanished across the pub yard.

'See!' Walter said, laughing again. He picked up the bike. 'Nothing's safe with our Tom on the scene!' He turned to Mandy, then he looked down the row to Ernie's end house. 'But you know something, I think we've just had an idea!'

'We have?' To Mandy it didn't feel as if anything was going right.

'Yes. You hit it off with old Ernie, didn't you?' Walter scratched his head; a sure sign that he was thinking.

'I suppose so,' Mandy said doubtfully. 'Listen, you don't think I should ask him!' Her eyes lit up. 'I mean, you mean I should ask him to take a kitten!' She felt the idea light up all the dark corners of her mind.

But Walter was shaking his head. 'No, no, I don't think you should ask him exactly!'

Mandy's face fell again. 'Why not? He likes animals. He rescued little Sammy, didn't he?'

'Yes, but Ernie would say no if you asked him directly. On principle, he always says no. He's a grumpy, cantankerous old so-and-so, is Ernie.'

Mandy had to agree. 'So what's our idea?' she asked.

'It's this!' Walter got into a huddle with Mandy round the corner, out of sight.

The idea involved taking a very big risk. But then Mandy had forty-eight hours to solve four very big problems. She listened to Walter, she nodded, she considered it. She thought of Sammy snug in his custom-built hutch. She decided to risk it.

So she rang home and said she'd be late. Then she rode back over to Walton.

Mrs Williams watched with concern as Mandy gave Amy a special feed and tucked her into a specially lined cardboard box. Amy peered up, unseeing, sniffed, then settled down. Walton came over, glanced in, looked up at Mandy, then retreated to the laundry basket. She sat quietly inside with her other three kittens, looking out.

'She trusts you!' Mrs Williams said. 'Poor lamb, she trusts you with her babies!'

Mandy nodded. It was a hard thing to do, to take the kitten from her mother, but it was a hard thing Mr Williams was threatening to do, and Walter's plan made it necessary. 'Good girl, Walton,' she said. Carefully she folded down the flaps of the cardboard box.

'I hope you know what you're doing!' Mrs Williams whispered.

Mandy looked her in the face. Her heart was in her mouth as she nodded and went outside. She strapped the box on to her bike, nodded again at Mrs Williams, tried not to think about Walton and the three cosy kittens in their basket, and set off across the moor.

It was the most heartstopping bike ride she'd ever made. Every bend, every hill she took at snail's pace. She came down into Welford holding her breath. She stopped at the pub, out of sight of Walter and Ernie's row of cottages. Then she unstrapped the box and crept with it in through Walter's open door.

'Got it?' Walter asked.

Mandy nodded. She opened the box. Amy mewed at the light. 'Are you sure this will work?' she asked again.

Walter's head went to one side. 'Not sure,' he said 'Not one hundred per cent.' He gazed down at tiny, helpless Amy. 'She's just a skinny little thing!' He tickled her head.

'Ernie's got a mind of his own. You can bet he'll do exactly the opposite to what you ask. Always has. You say to him, "Ernie, do me a favour, fix the latch on this back gate for me," and he'll say straight back, "What do you think I am, the odd-jobman round here?" and he'll stamp off in the other direction. But if he thinks it's his idea and he sees your gate's broken, he'll make a point of coming up and he'll say, "I saw your latch needed mending, Walter, so I just got out my toolbag and fixed it for you." Just like that!'

Mandy understood. 'Like rescuing Sammy, you mean? It had to be his idea.' She lifted Amy out of her box. 'So if he finds a tiny kitten abandoned on his doorstep, he'll take her in?'

Walter nodded. 'As long as he does think it's his idea! Then he'll want to keep her and look after her, just like the squirrel. He'll come along to me for advice because he knows I've got the three cats, and I'll suggest, very cunning, how much better it'd be to find a feeding mother until the kitten's properly on its feet. That's where you come in, little miss!'

Mandy looked hard at Amy. 'Are you sure?'

He nodded again. 'Ernie's got a heart of gold, underneath it all!' Walter smiled. 'Go on, lass, what have you got to lose? That kitten will have a foster home and be back with her mother before you can say Jack Robinson!'

So Mandy took the precious bundle down the length of the row. Amy squirmed in her hands, mewing piteously. 'Shh!' she whispered. Could she do it? Mandy felt as if her heart would stop. Could she leave the poor little thing on a cold doorstep?

She almost stopped to retrace her steps. But what was the alternative? She had less than two days left. Forcing herself to go on, she stooped down by Ernie's front doorstep. She closed her eyes, backed away, and fled down to Walter's house.

'Now we just have to wait,' Walter said. They stood inside his doorway, listening to Amy's tiny wail.

'Oh, quick!' Mandy breathed. 'Please hear her and come quickly!'

But Ernie's door stayed shut.

Amy mewed her high-pitched sound. Would he hear it? They waited. Mandy leaned forward, desperately wanting to see if Amy was all right. But Walter pulled her back. 'You mustn't let him see you!' he warned.

The wait seemed endless. Minutes went by. Amy's
tiny howling continued.

Then finally they heard the metal bolts of Ernie's
door. They heard the latch turn. The door scraped
open. 'What the—!' Ernie said. He grunted as he
stooped. 'Oh-aagh!' They heard him sigh as he
picked up the kitten and straightened his old back.
He stepped out on to the path. He took time to look
up and down. He even carried Amy a few steps
towards Walter's house, then he turned and went
indoors, carrying the kitten.

'Well?' Mandy was still holding her breath. She
looked at Walter.

Walter listened. He considered carefully. Then he
brought up one hand in a thumbs-up sign. 'I reckon
it's worked!' he said.

They had to wait half an hour, maybe more, drinking tea and eating Rich Tea biscuits, before they heard Ernie shuffling down the path to Walter's door.

'Say nothing!' Walter warned. 'And stay here!'

Mandy nodded.

'Now then, Walter,' Ernie said. He poked his head inside the front door. 'You know about cats!'

'I do, Ernie,' Walter said. 'I know something about them, any rate.' Mandy sat out of sight in the back kitchen as Walter went down the hall to greet Ernie. 'Why, what have you got there?' He managed to sound genuinely surprised.

'Kitten,' Ernie said. 'What's it look like?' He had wrapped Amy in an old grey jumper. 'It's shivering.' He showed the little bundle to Walter.

'Aye, it would,' Walter said. 'It's only a littl'un.'

'It just turned up out of the blue,' Ernie said. 'I was just doing my washing-up when I heard it set up a racket on my doorstep! I reckon its mother dropped it there; one too many to look after in the litter!'

'Well, it must be your week for it,' Walter said, keeping his voice flat this time. 'First the squirrel, now this.'

'I dunno about that. It just turned up.' Ernie stood there looking helpless. Peeping, Mandy could see the

two old men, head to head against the square of light
in the doorway.

'Ah, well, I reckon you'll have to get rid of this
one,' Walter said. 'Two orphans to look after is more
than you can manage.'

Mandy gasped and bit her lip. How could he?
How could Walter take such a risk?

But Ernie gave Walter his eagle stare. 'What do
you mean, more than I can manage?' He wrapped
Amy up carefully. 'I've no intention of getting rid of
it, Walter Pickard! No, this little kitten is here to
stay!'

Mandy cried. She cried tears of silent joy.

'Aye, but how will you feed it? Look at it, poor
little scrap. It needs feeding already,' Walter insisted.

Ernie thought about this for a while. 'That's why
I'm coming to you, Walter. You know about cats.'

Now it was Walter's turn to stand there looking
awkward and sullen. 'It's too young for me to
handle. It needs a mother cat,' he said. 'One that's
still feeding her own youngsters.'

Ernie squared his shoulders and asked how they
would set about finding such a thing; a mother cat
that would feed his kitten until it was weaned? He'd
like Walter to ring the vet right then and there, on his
telephone, and get the vet's young girl over there as

quick as possible. 'I reckon she'll know of just such a cat,' Ernie said, hugging Amy to his chest.

'Oh, she'll know,' Walter confirmed, giving a little smile.

Back in the kitchen, Mandy grinned. Walter's plan had worked perfectly!

'Then you go ahead and give her a ring. You tell her I want her down at my cottage in fifteen minutes sharp!' Ernie instructed. 'And tell her to bring something to carry a tiny kitten in. We need a mother cat straight off, else my little kitten will starve to death!'

'Right!' Walter agreed.

'Right!' And Ernie marched on back home with Amy.

Walter came back grinning all over his face. Mandy sat on the kitchen stool and smiled through her tears. They'd found a home for Amy. At last they'd found one good home!'

Nine

Mandy paid a visit to Ernie's, complete with her lined cardboard box. She fed Amy quickly and expertly, mixing the powdered food in a miniature feeding bottle. She held Amy in one hand, then stroked her abdomen with a forefinger to help her digest the food and get rid of the waste. Ernie didn't bat an eyelid at that.

'You have to do it, otherwise, they hang on to it and get constipated,' Mandy explained. 'That's why the mother cats lick them.'

'And how often will this mother cat have to feed it?'

'*She* needs feeding every couple of hours. And the mother will keep her warm too,' Mandy said.

Ernie picked up his kitten and said an awkward goodbye. His fingers looked broad and clumsy against Amy's tiny head, but he held her calmly. He gave her every scrap of his attention. He bent his white head, making encouraging little chucking noises with his tongue. Then he looked up. 'I'll call her Tiddles!' he said.

Mandy started to protest, then bit her tongue hard. She couldn't tell Ernie that Amy already had a name. She swallowed and nodded. 'Good idea.' She took the kitten from Ernie and put her carefully in the box. 'She'll be ready to come home in six or seven weeks,' she promised.

So Amy became Tiddles. 'Brilliant name, isn't it?' She greeted James with the news when they met up in the village early next morning. But Mandy was so thrilled that the name hardly mattered. 'Three more to go!' she said, full of new enthusiasm for the task. The morning was sunny. Things had begun to go right.

James nodded. He was looking pale and tired.

'What's wrong?' Mandy asked. She was peering in through the post office window to make sure that their card was still up there on the notice-board.

'Nothing.' James shook his head, and made ready to set off for school. He refused to look Mandy in the face as he mumbled, 'Let's go.'

'No, there is something wrong!' Mandy insisted. James was always shy and only ever got visibly excited about football. But today there was something making him even quieter than usual. He hadn't really reacted to the news about Amy. He hadn't said, Great. Well done. I knew you could do it, Mandy!

James shook his head again. He was staring down at his trainers.

Mandy put one hand on the handlebar of his bike. 'It's Benji, isn't it?' she said softly.

And James nodded.

'Oh, James, what's wrong with him?' She could have kicked herself. She'd been so full of her own news that she'd forgotten all about poor Benji being ill.

But James couldn't speak. He just sighed.

'He's going to be all right, isn't he? I mean they'll sort him out down at the Ark. It isn't anything serious, is it? What did my mum and dad say?' Mandy was beginning to sense something really awful. She'd never seen James look so sad.

And finally he came out with it. 'Benji's dead,' he said. 'We had to have him put down.'

Mandy gasped. She expected the whole sky to come crashing down. Benji was dead. 'Why?' She couldn't believe it.

The story came pouring out now. 'He had some kind of tumour on his brain. We didn't know it was anything serious, only over the weekend he was a bit groggy. Off his food and so on.' James paused to take a deep breath. 'He kept staggering. My dad laughed and said he must have been out on Saturday night drinking. He looked pretty sorry for himself, so my mum said we'd take him into the Ark.' He paused again and glanced at Mandy. 'I think my mum knew,' he said.

She nodded. 'Then what?' No more Benji, she was thinking. No more Benji curled up on a seat in the Hunters' conservatory. No more Benji leaping from the sloping roof up through the bathroom window. Benji had always been there. He was part of the Hunter family.

James shrugged. He stared hard at his feet again. He was standing astride his bike, head down, miserable. 'My mum took him in yesterday. By that time he could hardly stand. It was your mum who looked at him.' Mandy realised that nothing in

James's life had ever been so difficult for him to say. 'Anyway, she said he had this growth on his brain. And there was nothing to be done in this kind of case.'

'So?'

He sniffed. 'So your mum explained that he'd be in a lot of pain.'

'And *your* mum agreed to have him put to sleep?'

James nodded. 'It would have been cruel to let him live.'

For a second Mandy's hand touched James's. 'That's true,' she said.

Then there was a big silence. They both thought of Benji. Patient old Benji who'd grown up with them, who'd always let you pick him up any old how, and who always sat on your lap and let you tickle his chin. He'd put up over the years with all their rough treatment, and he'd never put in a cross word. He was a great cat.

'Let's go!' James said. He glanced round at Mandy. 'I told my mum to tell them at the Ark not to say anything to you about it. I wanted to tell you myself.'

Mandy nodded and followed on. Life, like the road over to Walton, was full of ups and downs.

It must have been hard for James, she thought, to

help with the kittens this morning. He did the jobs as usual, before school and during lunch break. He listened as Mandy told Mrs Williams how Amy, alias Tiddles, was safely back with Walton. And her future was secure.

'I hope this Ernie Bell person knows what he's doing with this kitten!' Mrs Williams said primly. 'I mean, men! They don't know how to look after things properly. They're not made that way!'

Mandy raised her eyebrows and glanced at James. He was busy with Smoky's feed. 'Oh, I don't know about that,' she said.

'Not my Eric, at least,' Mrs Williams blundered on. 'Mind you, he's a bit old-fashioned in that respect.'

As if on cue, Mr Williams tramped in for his lunch. He ate in silence, glancing sullenly at the kitten activity in the far corner of the kitchen. 'Tomorrow's D-Day!' he reminded them as he reached for his cap. 'And don't you forget!'

D-Day. Death Day. Destruction Day. Deadline Day. Mandy didn't think it was possible to hate someone as much as she hated Mr Williams just then. He stamped off down the garden path, tweaking a rose bush, perking up a primula.

'He's got to go and see the Headmaster!' Mrs

Williams whispered to Mandy. 'He's had the summons!'

Mandy raised her head. She couldn't help that, she thought. And all she really cared about right now was the kitten problem.

'Do you want to go straight on home after school?' she asked James, on their way into afternoon lessons. She thought there was only so much she could ask him to do, considering Benji.

James looked up at the school shield in the entrance hall. Underneath there was a list of names of men who'd died in two wars, and underneath that was the school motto: 'Through Suffering We Succeed!'

'No,' he said to Mandy. 'I'll be there as usual!'

James must have been thinking about poor Benji all through his games afternoon. Mandy had glanced out of the science lab window down on to the sports field, and she'd spotted him hanging about miserably on the touchline, most unlike him.

But when they met up after school, his face looked composed, even calm. 'I just want to ring my mum,' he told her. 'I'll be across in a minute.'

So Mandy went on ahead. As usual, the routine of caring for the kittens took over and she managed to push away the worry about James. She watched with delight their fluffy, wriggling little bodies, their ears beginning to unfold and perk up into position, their bruising battle to feed and to survive.

James came in just as she lifted Eric out of the basket for his feed. She handed the kitten to him. 'Here, you do Eric,' she said.

They worked in silence for a few minutes. Then James pushed his glasses up the bridge of his nose, sat back and made an announcement. 'I'd like Eric!' He said it quite straightforwardly, just like, 'I'd like a Mars bar!' or, 'Tea with milk but no sugar, please!'

Mandy stared. 'What did you say?'

'I'd like Eric,' he repeated. 'I've thought about it, and I'd like to adopt Eric!'

'Are you sure?' Mandy put Smoky back into the basket. 'I mean you're sure it's not too soon after . . . I mean, well, are you *sure*?'

'Yes. I rang my mum. She agrees. If we're going to get another cat after Benji, we should do it straight away.' He looked down, half sad, half happy at the new scrap of life on his lap. 'And I'm sure Benji wouldn't mind!'

Mandy waltzed around the kitchen. 'Oh, great!' she said. 'You hear that, Walton? Oh, brilliant! Oh, James!' She smiled and smiled.

Walton mewed.

There were practical things to arrange. When Mr Williams threw the kittens out next day, should James take Eric home then, or could they work out a way to keep Walton and the kittens together until they were weaned? A halfway house. That was the thing to work on, Mandy told James. She looked at Mrs Williams, who was hovering in the doorway with her shopping basket.

'Don't ask me!' she muttered darkly. 'Eric is in with the Headmaster this very minute. Lord knows what's going to happen to any of us!' She went out tight-lipped, shaking her head.

'It's something we can work on,' Mandy told James as they went out to their bicycles. 'A halfway house. Anyway, we've got two good homes. Two brilliant homes!' Mandy could have sung for joy as they rode home.

'Two to go!' Mandy told her mum as she flung her schoolbag in the corner of the hallway. She told her about James's decision to take Eric. 'He's probably the grumpiest kitten of them all, like the person he's named after,' she joked. 'But James seems to like him!'

Mrs Hope smiled. 'He's a good boy.' Then she

asked Mandy to help in the kitchen. 'Your dad's out on an emergency call. One of Mrs Janeki's sheep. But your grandad rang while you were out, just to let us know they're back.'

Mandy nodded. 'Did they have a good time?'

'He didn't say. But he said your gran had got a reply from the Prime Minister.' Mrs Hope looked puzzled. 'Could that be right?'

'Yes. But that was quick.' Mandy asked if she could run up to see them.

'After supper,' Mrs Hope said. She always had to remind her daughter to slow down enough to eat. 'What's the point of me preparing all these vegetarian meals for you if you won't even sit down and eat one!' she complained.

Mandy gave her a hug. 'OK, Mum, after supper!'

The camper van sat in the driveway, splashed but splendid. 'Hi, Gran! Hi, Grandad!' Mandy burst in on them. She reported the good news about Tiddles ('What a name!') and Eric. She said James was a hero, a real hero!

'Oho!' her grandad raised his eyebrows.

'No, Grandad, not like that!' she said.

'That's what they always say. I think Mandy's got a soft spot for young James.'

'Stop teasing, Thomas!' Mandy's gran warned. 'Anyway, she's come to see my letter from the Prime Minister, haven't you, love!'

Mandy nodded and laughed. 'Sorry, Gran. It's just that the kittens have been taking up all my time. Did you have a good holiday?' she remembered to ask.

There was a small silence. 'Yes,' Gran said. 'But about this letter from 10 Downing Street. See, official notepaper!' She waved the reply in Mandy's face.

'"Yes" means "Yes, but!",' Grandad put in. 'And then we quickly change the subject!'

'Why, what happened? Did the camper break down?'

'Break down!' he exclaimed. 'You must be joking!'

'Of course not,' Mrs Hope said. 'The camper was perfect. But Scarborough wasn't.'

'Not sunny?'

'Sodden,' Mrs Hope conceded. 'Forty-two hours of solid rain. We counted!'

'Ah,' Mandy said. 'What a shame.'

'Yes, but this letter here, see!' Gran waved it before starting to read:

'"Dear Mrs Hope,
    The Prime Minister acknowledges receipt of

your letter. While he recognises your concern
about the continued existence of your local sub
post office, he wishes me to point out that
Government policy on the issue is the concern of
one of his junior ministers.

    Accordingly he has asked me to pass on this
matter to the relevant department.

             Yours sincerely,

             E.B.Whyte

             (Assistant private secretary to

                   the Prime Minister)''

'There!' Mrs Hope flung the cream-coloured letter
on to the table.

    'What does it mean?' Mandy asked. 'Are they
going to close McFarlane's or not?'

    'It doesn't mean yes, it doesn't mean no. It doesn't
mean anything!' Gran said indignantly.

    'It means they've passed the buck,' Grandad said.
'As usual.'

    'They won't get away with it!' Gran insisted.

    Grandad muttered in a stage whisper, 'Watch it,
love, she's on the warpath!'

    Gran ignored him. 'We'll have a campaign. Save
our post office!' She stood up and strode across the
room.

Mandy was enjoying this; her gran on her high horse.

'I'll have to organise everything, of course!' There was a glint in Gran's eye.

Bells began to ring in Mandy's head. In fact, they set up a giant racket! Did this mean her grandparents would have to put their feet firmly back on Welford ground?

'This'll take a lot of time and energy, Gran,' she pointed out.

'Who cares?' Gran swept around the room. 'It's important! In fact, it's vital! We'll design a logo for our campaign. A heart shape, to show our post office is at the heart of the village!' Her hair was coming loose from its comb and she was looking very fiery.

'I'm glad I'm not the poor little Prime Minister!' Grandad laughed.

'Does this mean you might not go to Portugal?' Mandy asked. 'I mean, you might have to stay at home more to run this campaign.'

Gran stopped in her paces. Grandad said, 'Ha!'

'We-ell,' Gran said. 'We might not go quite so far afield as we thought.' She gave Mandy a little grin. 'The fact is, we missed you all terribly; you and your mum and dad, and this old place!' She sighed. 'We're a pair of old softies, after all!'

'And then there's my tomatoes to consider,' Grandad said thoughtfully. 'I'll have to talk nicely to my tomatoes!'

Mandy looked at them, bursting to put the question. She took a great, deep breath. 'Does this mean you might be willing to take a kitten after all?'

They broke into smiles, both of them. They hugged her. 'We thought you'd never ask!' They looked at each other. Clearly they'd been thinking about it all the time they'd been away in soggy Scarborough.

'Smoky!' Mandy said, breathless.

'On two conditions,' Gran added.

'What?' She glowed with happiness. A home for the third kitten. A home just up the hill from Animal Ark. Mandy couldn't believe it.

'First, you've got to agree to come up and feed him whenever we do go away for a couple of days,' Gran said. 'When we go off in the camper to lovely Llandudno or wherever.'

This was hardly a condition! Mandy nodded, speechless. She'd love to feed Smoky. Then he'd be half hers, wouldn't he! She just sat there nodding.

'Second!' Grandad said, frowning and trying to look serious. 'You must swear to water my tomatoes!'

'Oh, yes,' she said. She'd even talk to them. 'Oh, yes, yes!'

Ten

Thursday came, and Mandy woke three quarters happy, one quarter sad. Her heart felt pulled apart over Patch; poor little Patch, the only kitten still left homeless.

Mrs Hope looked at her across the breakfast table. 'Problem?' she asked.

'You realise what day it is,' Mandy said miserably.

'Thursday,' her father said helpfully over the top of his newspaper.

'Yes, Thursday. And I've found homes for three of the kittens in Mr Williams's kitchen, but there's still one left over! Today's the deadline!' The word 'deadline' had an awful hollow ring.

'Hasn't the mother cat decided to move off to a new nest site yet?' Mr Hope asked.

Mandy shook her head. 'No, she's still there in the kitchen, in the laundry basket. And today's the day *he* throws them out!'

'You mean Mr Williams,' Mrs Hope corrected her. 'Not "he". So what next?'

'Gran and Grandad say they don't mind if the kittens and Walton move in with them until the kittens are weaned in about six weeks time.' Mandy managed a smile of relief. It had been a close thing all round.

'But?' Mrs Hope asked.

'But they say the same thing as you. They say I have to find a home for Patch. Otherwise it's cruel to keep him alive!' Her eyes filled. 'Poor Patch!'

'It's true. You can't just turn him out to fend for himself when the time comes. He has to have a home!' Even her soft-hearted father was telling her the same thing; the thing she didn't want to hear.

'Dad!' she cried.

'There's no "Dad!" about it,' Mrs Hope said firmly. 'Look, Mandy, you've done brilliantly to find these three homes. We think you're wonderful!'

'Don't!' The tears brimmed over and down her cheeks.

Mrs Hope looked across at Mr Hope. Mandy thought she spied a glimmer of hope through her tears. 'Listen, love, I'll come across and see you at school this lunchtime, all right?'

'What for?' Mandy said, sniffing and drying her eyes.

'Wait and see. I can't promise anything yet.' Mrs Hope smiled and patted Mandy's hand. 'Just wait and see.'

That lunchtime Mandy fed Patch with an aching heart. James was busy with little Eric, and the other two kittens were already snuggled down in the basket, when there was a knock at the door.

'Hello. Is Mandy here?' a voice said to Mrs Williams.

She recognised her mum, but the misery of looking down at Patch's little face, his eyes nearly open now, was too much. She couldn't bear to think about what might have to happen to him.

'Mandy?' her mum's voice said again.

She looked up.

'I've brought someone with me. Mrs Hope was gentle but firm, as always. 'Come in, and let's have a look at this little fellow.'

Mandy felt suddenly surrounded by people and

dragged back to the present from fears of the future. She pulled herself together. 'Sorry,' she said, standing up with Patch cupped in her hands. Her eyes focused on the visitors: Miss Marjorie and Miss Joan Spry!

What on earth was Mrs Hope up to? Mandy stood up, ready to protest, but her mum gave her a meaningful look.

'This is the kitten Mandy came to see you about,' Mrs Hope explained calmly. 'And I'm sure she apologises for running off so rudely.' She smiled encouragingly at Mandy, who went red and nodded without saying anything.

The two sisters nodded back and peered down at Patch. They poked their thin faces towards him curiously. They looked silently at each other.

Mandy had got over her shock. She trusted her mum to know what she was doing. And today the Spry twins didn't look so strange. Their untidy hair was combed back underneath straw hats, and their pastel summer coats made them look like quaint wedding guests.

'This is the only kitten left without a home,' Mandy said. She offered Patch to one of the twins, not knowing which one.

The twin shook her head. 'No, give him to Joan.

See if she likes him,' Miss Marjorie said. 'She did promise to try and like him!'

Mandy held out the kitten again. With shaking hands Miss Joan took the little fur scrap and cradled it. She brought her face close to the kitten's and felt it lick her finger. 'What is its name?' she breathed.

'Patch,' Mandy said, holding her own breath. 'He's just one week old!'

Joan looked up at her sister. The silence held them all like a net. Would she say yes? Would she give Patch a home and a future?

'Yes,' she said at last. 'I think I like him!'

'Of course you do! What did I tell you!' Miss Marjorie said.

And they all smiled and congratulated one another. They listened to Mandy's instructions about how a kitten should be treated: 'Don't poke him, don't press him too hard, don't disturb him too much!' She said they should put him back with his mother now. 'The excitement's too much for him,' she said as she returned a squeaking Patch to his warm, dark nest.

The Spry twins smiled and thanked Mandy and went off happily through the porch, arm in arm.

'See!' Mrs Hope said, head to one side. 'Didn't I say they were harmless? You have to learn that all people are different, but that doesn't make them wrong. This kitten will be the best thing that's happened to the twins in an awfully long time!'

Mandy laughed and hugged her mum. 'Oh, thanks!' she said. A great weight had lifted off her chest. She sighed and looked in on the kittens. They were curled up, snug and warm against Walton's sleeping body. 'Four homes! We did it!'

'*You* did it,' Mrs Hope said. 'You and James!'

They looked at each other with huge grins on their faces. James went red, even before Mandy hugged him.

When Miss Marjorie came back in for a moment, James leapt back. Dainty as a canary in her pale yellow coat, she made straight for Mandy. 'Thank you, my dear!' she said, patting her hand. 'Thank you for bringing life back into our dark, dreary house. It's all due to you!' She beamed, nodded lightly at James. 'I'd best get back to my sister. We'll wait for you in the car,' she told Mrs Hope before tripping off again.

'Happy now?' Mandy's mum asked.

Her eyes shone with tears again. She nodded and they nearly spilled over. This time Mandy could say nothing at all!

*　*　*

Afternoon school ended and the great move began. 'It's time for a new nest, Walton,' Mandy told her gently. 'And you don't even have to do it yourself, you lucky cat!'

'You're sure it'll be all right now?' Mrs Williams fussed. There was no sign of her husband. It was a heavy day, threatening rain when Mandy's grand-parents' camper van pulled up in the playground. 'Walton won't desert these kittens now?' She stood at the kitchen sink, grasping a tea towel.

'No, it'll work out OK, Mrs Williams. Don't worry!' Mandy looked up and realised the old lady would miss Walton and the kittens after all. She smiled. 'Honestly, Walton would fight to the death for them now. She's made a good strong bond with them. Thanks to you, of course!'

'Oh!' Mrs Williams raised her hands and smiled modestly.

'Yes, you gave them a good start. Now my gran and grandad will keep a close eye on them up at Lilac Cottage!'

'Then what?' Mrs Williams folded her tea towel into a precise rectangle. She laid it down on the draining-board and smoothed it carefully.

'Then James will take Eric and give him a home,' Mandy said, handing the kitten to him.

'And me and my wife will keep this little chap,' Grandad said, lifting Smoky in one hand.

'Ernie Bell is waiting to have Amy — er — Tiddles. And now Patch has found a home at The Riddings!' Mandy counted them off on her fingers.

Mrs Williams sniffed and nodded. 'And what about Walton?'

Mandy looked at James. 'We haven't got that far!'

He shrugged. 'We've got a bit of time to sort it out.'

'Well, I'll have to have a word with my Eric,' Mrs Williams said. But she would say no more.

So they drove off in triumph in the silver camper; cat and kittens, James, Mandy and her grandad.

Walton quickly regained her strength in the sunny warmth of Lilac Cottage. After three more weeks Smoky, Patch, Tiddles and Eric began to bounce and tumble. They chased anything that moved. On Mr Hope's lawn they sat in wait for butterflies to land on the purple buddleia. Still as statues, they watched and waited. Then they bounced and pounced and tumbled. They always missed. They turned endless somersaults. Mandy would score them out of ten like international gymnasts doing their floor exercises.

James came often to check on Eric. He lay propped

on his elbows out on the lawn, with a computer magazine spread out in front of him. He pretended to read, but really he watched Eric's every move; his grumpy swipes with his front paws at mischievous Smoky and Patch, his sulking under the shade of the rhubarb leaves.

'Don't worry,' Mandy said. 'After a week in your house he'll be as sweet-tempered and patient as poor old Benji was. It's the Hunters' magic way with cats!'

James looked up from his magazine and smiled.

Mandy went down regularly to the village to report to Ernie on Tiddles's progress. Ernie would ask endless questions about his kitten and waited with

utter impatience for the day when he could have her
home. 'Hey!' he warned Sammy, flipping the
squirrel off his shoulder. 'Stop nipping my ear, you!'
The squirrel, who had free range of Ernie's kitchen,
scampered down his back and round his waist, to
cling on to his belt buckle.

Mandy laughed. 'He'll be jealous when Tiddles
comes!'

'And so he should be,' Ernie said. 'I can't wait to
get that kitten home!'

At Lilac Cottage, Walton fed the four kittens less
and less, watched them take to solid food and grew
rather bored with motherhood. These days she
preferred a quiet corner in the kitchen underneath
the vegetable rack, with a bit of peace and quiet. Her
job was almost done.

Half-term holiday arrived. It was a green world;
everyone was packing up and going home.

'Now, then,' Mr Williams grunted at Mandy by
way of greeting. She was unlocking the padlock on
her bike.

She glanced up. It was unusual for the caretaker to
talk to her at all these days, and it was weeks since
she'd seen his wife. 'Oh, great!' she muttered.

She hadn't forgiven him for hanging that dreadful

threat over their heads, even though things had worked out fine in the end. The best she could do was to avoid the caretaker whenever possible. She hastily got ready to push off for home.

'How are those kittens of yours?' Mr Williams grumbled in his low, gravelly voice. 'Getting pretty big and strong by now, I should think?'

Mandy nodded.

'And I hear you've found folk willing to take them on?' he persisted. One hand was on his precious garden gate, but he looked like a man with something on his mind.

Oh, go away, just go away! Mandy thought to herself.

But instead he said, 'Come here a second,' and looked round furtively at the lace curtains of the kitchen window. 'I want to have a word!'

It involved Mandy riding back to school on the first day of her half-term holiday. She had the basket strapped carefully to the back of her bike. *Who would have believed it?* she thought to herself as she lifted the basket, reached in, and gathered Walton gently in her arms.

'Come on, Walton, come on girl!' she murmured.

'Shh!' said Mr Williams, gesturing towards the porch. 'This is still a secret!'

Mandy nodded and set Walton down. Immaculate, ladylike, and elegant as a model on a catwalk, Walton sniffed the logs, tested the doormat, pushed the door with her paw. It swung open.

'Eric?' Mrs Williams called from inside the kitchen. Mandy grinned at the caretaker. Then, 'Eric!' Mrs Williams said again, her voice high-pitched and surprised. 'Eric, this cat has just walked back into this kitchen as if she owns the place!'

They went inside to see, and there was Mrs Williams staring down at the familiar black and white shape. 'How did she get here? Did she walk?' Mrs Williams demanded.

Her husband gave a self-conscious little laugh. 'No, as a matter of fact, Amy, I asked this young lady here to bring her back home for you!'

Mrs Williams looked up at him, her eyes filling with tears. 'Oh, Eric!'

'Aye, well!' He looked embarrassed. 'I knew you were pining for the daft cat.' He half turned towards Mandy. 'She nattered me to death about it! She's too soft by half, my wife!'

Mandy watched Walton wrap herself around Mrs Williams's legs, purring like mad. She peered in her corner for food and looked up as if to say, 'Where is it, then?' They laughed, gave her a saucer of milk and made a great fuss of her homecoming.

'And will we take her with us?' Mrs Williams asked, still unable to believe her husband's change of heart.

'Why, where are you going?' Mandy asked.

'Eric's leaving his job.'

'He's not . . .?' Mandy looked anxiously at the old couple. Had Mr Williams's arthritis finally beaten him?

'No, he's not got the sack,' Mrs Williams said. 'No, in fact the Headmaster only wanted to see him to ask him to stay on beyond retirement age. He said he'd never find another caretaker as good as Eric!'

Mr Williams tut-tutted.

'Yes, he did, Eric! But he came home and we talked about it, and we decided of our own accord that we'd call it a day. We're getting on a bit and we want some peace and quiet in our old age.'

Mr Williams nodded. He watched Walton grooming herself after her drink. She was sitting on the window-sill, using her front paw to clean behind her ears. 'Well!' he said, taken aback.

'I told you they're nice clean animals!' Mandy laughed.

'So we've decided to retire!' Mrs Williams announced. 'We've got our eye on one of the new bungalows just up the road!'

'A quiet little cul-de-sac, plenty of garden!' Mr Williams said.

'Perfect for Walton?' Mandy could hardly keep the smile from spreading all over her face.

The caretaker looked at his wife and broke into a grin. 'I suppose so,' he said, shaking his head.

'And will it be all right if I book Walton in at Animal Ark for her operation?' Mandy asked, trying to be tactful.

'Operation?' Mr Williams repeated slowly.

'Yes, so she won't have any more kittens.'

'Oh,' he said, very old-fashioned. '*That* operation!'

'Yes, you don't want any more little ones cluttering up your kitchen, getting in amongst your best shirts!'

Mr Williams went bright red. He looked sheepishly at his wife, then his face broke into a broad grin again. 'I should say not!' he agreed.

So Mandy made the arrangements. She wouldn't hear of them having to pay for Walton being spayed. She knew her mum and dad would want that too. So she said she would book Walton in for the following Monday. Mandy took the hand offered by Mr Williams and shook it warmly.

'No hard feelings?' he asked.

'None!' she said.

*   *   *

Mandy rode home along the moor road. She felt on top of the world, literally. The road crested the hill. Lapwings curved overhead in the clear sky, the moor rolled in every direction. Perfect!

She headed downhill to Welford and Animal Ark. She'd go in to see who else needed rescuing; maybe a lost hedgehog who'd found its way to the surgery, or a 'male' hamster who'd just produced six babies! ('The pet shop said it was a boy, they did really!')

The wind caught Mandy's hair. She tilted her head back and stuck her legs out sideways to freewheel down the hill. And she laughed out loud.

LUCY DANIELS

Bunnies
—*in the*—
Bathroom

Illustrations by Shelagh McNicholas

*Hodder
Children's
Books*

a division of Hodder Headline plc

Bunnies in the Bathroom

Special thanks to Jenny Oldfield

Text copyright © Ben M. Baglio 1995
Created by Ben M. Baglio, London W6 0HE
Illustrations copyright © Shelagh McNicholas 1995

First published as a single volume in Great Britain in 1995
by Hodder Children's Books

One

'James, come and look at these!' Mandy Hope hovered over a counter full of chocolate bunnies, all wrapped in cellophane and tied up with pink, yellow and blue ribbons. Rows of little rabbits crouched, looking up at her with their enormous almond-shaped eyes. Their ears seemed to twitch. 'They're so lifelike!' she whispered.

James Hunter sighed. 'Uh-oh, I can see this is going to be your newest craze. Rabbits!'

'What's wrong with that?' Mandy knew he was teasing. 'It's nearly Easter, isn't it? Easter bunnies!'

'Yes, well, they're better than boring old eggs, I

suppose,' James grumbled. He joined Mandy at the counter. There were rows of fat chocolate pigs beside the shy bunnies, and some cheerful frogs squatting, dark brown and shiny, along the back of the counter.

'Yes, please?' Mr Cecil said, coming out from the back room. He brought with him the delicious bittersweet smell of melted chocolate. He wore a spotless white coat and sparkling, silver-rimmed spectacles. His head was round and bald and shiny. 'Can I help?'

Mandy took ages to decide. She wanted a small gift for each of her friends in Welford village: for Jean Knox who worked as the receptionist at Animal Ark; for Simon, their nurse; for Lydia Fawcett on the goat farm up at High Cross; and for Ernie Bell in the cottages behind the Fox and Goose pub.

'Do you do squirrels?' she asked Mr Cecil. A squirrel would be ideal for Ernie, who had his own pet squirrel in a run in his back garden.

'Squirrels? Certainly.' The old man spread his hands to display the bushy-tailed creatures. Each clutched a hazelnut in its front paws. 'In dark chocolate, milk chocolate, or white chocolate?' he asked.

Mandy hesitated again. 'Oh!' she sighed. 'They're all so . . . perfect!'

'Frogs for me,' James decided in an instant. He pointed to the comical shapes, all squatting on their haunches, their mouths stretched wide. He ordered six in milk chocolate and waited for Mr Cecil to pack them into a white cardboard box with 'Cecil's Confectionery' printed in elegant silver letters on the top and sides.

'Of course, they'd be too good to eat.' Mandy switched her gaze back to the baby rabbits. She peered once more through the glass counter and took a deep breath. 'I'll take a squirrel for Ernie, please, a pig for Simon, a frog for Jean, oh – and a bunny for Lydia!' She'd made up her mind at last.

'She'll love you for that!' James warned with a wry grin.

'Why?'

'Her fields are overrun with them. She's always going on about it. Rabbits make such a mess of the land.'

'But Lydia likes them all the same.' Mandy smiled across at her best friend. He looked so serious sometimes, with his glasses and his floppy fringe of dark brown hair. She turned to the shopkeeper. 'I don't suppose you do goats, by any chance?' she said suddenly.

Mr Cecil smiled and his eyes twinkled. 'No, I'm sorry. Their legs are too thin; they'd break. The same with horses, I'm afraid. Now, did you want this little chap in dark, milk, or white?' He pointed to the row of enchanting bunnies.

At last, the big decisions were made and all Mandy's little chocolate animals were safely packed inside a second cardboard box. Then the kind old man smiled and gestured for them to wait. 'I think you'd like to take a peek at something I've just finished,' he whispered. 'And I must say I'm rather pleased with it myself!'

Mandy balanced her light box with both hands and waited for him to return. He came back through the swing-doors, proudly displaying his latest masterpiece. It sat on an icing-sugar nest on a silver cardboard disc about thirty centimetres wide; a huge, glossy, chocolate hen, perfect in every detail, down to her beady eye and last wing feather. When Mandy looked more closely, she saw tiny white chocolate chicks peering out of the nest, and when Mr Cecil lifted the broody hen, there were the discarded shells and three more chocolate eggs with a pale brown sugar coating,

speckled and looking as though they were about
to hatch.

'Wow!' Even James allowed himself to be
impressed.

Mandy was speechless. Her eyes darted over the
beautiful, delicious object.

'Special order,' Mr Cecil said proudly. 'For Mrs
Parker Smythe. It's an Easter gift for her little girl,
Imogen.'

'Lucky thing!' Mandy breathed. She secretly
thought that spoilt Imogen Parker Smythe, who
lived in luxury up at Beacon House, just above
Welford village, had done nothing to deserve such

a special gift. She was a girl who had everything but seemed pleased with none of it.

Mr Cecil glanced across at Mandy. 'You like animals?' He nodded and smiled as she pored over the hen and her brood.

'Ha!' James laughed. 'You could say that!'

'I live at Animal Ark,' Mandy explained. 'My mum and dad are the Welford vets.'

'Ah!' The old man looked up as the doorbell gave a high, tuneful tinkle. Another customer had come into the shop. 'In that case, you'd be interested in the new pet shop that's just opened down the road.'

No sooner said than Mandy shot out on to the street, ahead of James, gabbling her thanks as she went.

James followed. 'Mandy, we have to catch the bus, remember!' He called after her. 'I promised my mum I'd be back home for tea.'

Mandy ran as fast as the precious box allowed her to, down Walton's main street with its rows of smart shop fronts, its cafés and bookshops. 'Just two minutes!' she shouted. 'I think we can still make it!'

She spotted the new pet shop and dashed over to peer through the window. At first she saw only her own reflection; a tall, slim figure in jeans and a sweater, with shortish blonde hair. Then, she made out racks of dog leads, furry playthings for kittens, imitation bones for dogs to chew, packs of dry rabbit food, budgerigar cages, and, at the back of the dark shop, a big glass aquarium with fish darting back and forth; vivid streaks of silver, blue and fiery red.

'Here comes the bus!' James warned.

'Hang on a sec!' The pet shop owner was carrying a bulky cage towards the window, coming out of the gloom of a back room. Struggling, he reached over a ledge and set it firmly in a space in the crowded window, in full view. The cage was lined with fresh straw. There was a clear drinking bottle tilted towards the floor, and when the cage was firmly settled and the warmth of the late sun struck through the glass of the shop window, Mandy saw a small movement. 'Look!' she whispered.

James instantly forgot all about the approaching bus. 'What is it?' He craned forward to look.

Two noses emerged from the more private wooden section, through a hole in the side. They were small, round and brown, with long whiskers. Then the ears came into view, erect and twitching; listening, listening.

'Baby rabbits!' Mandy breathed.

Two small, furry shapes shyly hopped into view. One sat and scratched his ears with his back leg, the other perched upright, his nose twitching. Then he came to the water bottle and began to drink, ears back, eyes still wide and staring.

'They're so perfect!' James marvelled at the tiny creatures. The second baby came to crouch in the sun, side by side, fawn-coloured and adorable, with great, liquid, dark eyes. 'But you've got three rabbits at home,' he reminded her. 'So don't get any ideas.' He glanced up at the name of the new shop; 'Pets' Parlour', written in bright red and gold letters.

'But *you* haven't!' Mandy turned sideways and widened her blue eyes in his direction. 'James . . .'

'No!' He jumped in quickly. 'Blackie and Eric are already a handful!' But he sighed all the same. The baby rabbits were irresistible. Still, Blackie, his Labrador, needed a lot of walking to keep his weight down, and Eric the kitten was into everything.

'Do you think someone nice will come along and buy them?' she asked with a touch of regret. She yearned to take them home, yet she knew that common sense said no. Animal Ark was always overflowing with visitors and patients; anything from Jack Russells with mites in their ears, to badgers wounded in traps.

'They're bound to,' James reassured her.

'I just hope they buy both of them together. Rabbits like company.' Slowly she stood back from the shop window. She smiled briefly at the owner; a tall young man in a dark blue sweater, with a red checked shirt.

'Mandy!' James reminded her about the time. He heard the bus engine choke and roar at the stop on the other side of the street.

Mandy stepped back again. 'Bye, bunnies!' she said wistfully. The two babies took slow, identical, rocking hops across their cage and sat, ears up, noses twitching.

'Don't worry, they'll find a good home,' James said as they crossed the busy street. They climbed on to the bus just as the driver let off the handbrake and signalled to pull out. He took their money and they sank into a nearby seat.

As the bus drew out of town and set off over the moor road towards Welford, Mandy found herself dreaming. Spring was in the air. The sticky-buds on the horse chestnut trees were beginning to burst open, the hawthorn hedges were tipped with green. In the fields, lambs nibbled at fresh young shoots or skipped up and down the hillside. She would have called those twin rabbits Barney and Button, she decided, and they would have the best food, with carrots and apples as a treat every weekend. She stared up at the drifting clouds as the bus rocked and swayed along the twisting road.

Gently James dug his elbow against her arm. 'Look!' He pointed out of the window.

The sun had sunk low, leaving the crest of the eastern hill bathed in warm, yellow light. Shadows fell long and deep over the rough pasture. In the distance there was a stretch of pale purple heather that ran all along the valley ridge. Nearby, in the soft sunlight, the green field was dotted with wild rabbits.

They sat in twos and threes; small brown shapes with pointed ears. At the sound of the bus they stamped their back legs and sniffed the air for danger. They looked startled, froze for a split second, then bolted. They fanned out across the field, scattering into the brambles and ditch bottoms. Some made for their underground runs. They vanished inside with a flash of white tail and one last kick of their powerful hind legs.

'Brilliant!' Mandy said. Then she turned to James. 'You were right!'

'What?' He blushed under her direct gaze.

'Today *is* the day for rabbits!' She held her box of chocolate animals safely on her knee as the bus jolted and lurched.

Two

The bus dropped them off outside the Fox and Goose. Mandy spotted Ernie Bell and his neighbour, Walter Pickard, sitting outside the pub. The two old men were chatting as usual on the porch by the front door of the low stone building. One either side of the door, they sat and watched whoever came and went.

'There you are!' Mandy went across with a bright smile.

'Where else?' Walter asked.

'Like a pair of bookends, we are,' Ernie agreed. 'You always know where to look for us on a fine night like this, sitting over a good pint, putting the world to rights. You can't beat it!' He took a sip from his glass, then pointed to Mandy's box. 'What've you got in there?'

'Aha, close your eyes!' Mandy replied. James joined her, and together they opened the boxes and took out one of the chocolate figures.

'Happy Easter!' they cried. Mandy presented a squirrel to Ernie and James gave a frog to Walter, who kept his eyes closed, his hands outstretched.

They opened their eyes. 'By gum!' Ernie said with a look at the squirrel. 'Lord knows what Sammy will make of this!' He gave Mandy a crooked, embarrassed smile.

'Well, I'll be . . . !' Walter's frog smiled up at him. 'He's a funny little fellow!'

'Don't you like them?' James was anxious not to offend the two old men. Walter was a cat lover; a steady, reliable friend to Mandy and James. Ernie seemed grumpier, with his low, growly voice and short, grey stubble. But adopting Sammy the squirrel and Tiddles the cat had softened him up, and ever since he'd always been willing to help them out of a tight corner.

Ernie sat and studied his cellophane-wrapped squirrel. 'What do I do with him? Eat him, or stick him on my mantelpiece?'

'Nay, the poor chap would melt by the fire!'
Walter put in. He grinned at James. 'Young sir,
you should never have gone to this trouble fo
old Ernie and me, you know!'

'Hey, hey, I'm not so old!' Ernie grumbled.
winked at Mandy. 'I reckon you've been i
Walton and paid a visit to Harry Cecil's posh s'
He's not cheap, I'm told. You shouldn't have
Walter says.'

His face set in a frown, but Mandy could
was pleased. She and James turned to lea
Walter half stood up from his bench and
them.

'Hang on a minute! What's this?'

A low, dark green car sped down the h
past the post office. It drew into the p
and the engine died.

'It's the boss!' Ernie said, meanin
the pub landlord. He called a warni
staff inside. 'Look lively! He's back

They heard empty glasses clink
the staff quickly removed them fr

'Didn't he go over to fetch his
afternoon?' Walter asked. He tur
seems to me young John Hardy i
when he goes inside!'

John had just got out of his father's car. He looked up at the pub, at the room where he lived with his father during the holidays. During term time he lived seventy or eighty kilometres away at Grange School in the Lake District.

James frowned, then turned to Mandy. 'Didn't his dad tell him about Sara?'

'Shh!' Walter warned.

Mandy widened her eyes and shook her head. John's dad, Julian, had announced his engagement just a week ago. His fiancée was one of the women who helped behind the bar.

'Just look at that whacking great suitcase,' Ernie pointed out. 'What's he got in there, the kitchen sink?'

Mandy saw Mr Hardy lift a case out of the boot. He let it thump heavily to the ground.

It was all too easy to forget about John Hardy when he was away at school. Mandy had known him all her life, yet never known him. That was the peculiar thing. He was eleven, the same age as James, and he was even born in the same week at Walton Maternity Hospital. He was a small, ordinary-looking boy, with dark, wavy hair that seemed to make his face rounder and a bit goody-goody. It was the sort of hair that always

stayed in place. He was never untidy, never hot, never running; always walking in his cool, collected manner. He looked more grown-up than eleven, but Mandy never thought he looked very happy.

'Come on, John,' his father said, leaving the suitcase where it was. He headed for the front door with eager steps. 'Leave that. I've got some news for you, and there's someone inside I want you to meet.' He smiled and went on ahead.

Mandy saw John hesitate. He was wearing a light Aran sweater and jeans. His white sports shoes looked brand-new, but somehow he looked as if he was in his Sunday best. Then Sara came to the door to greet them both. She looked nervous as she stood there waiting.

Ernie grunted, but Walter leaned across and jabbed him with his elbow. 'I'm saying nothing!' Ernie protested. But Mandy thought his sour look said plenty.

They watched uneasily as Sara clasped her hands in front of her.

'John, this is Sara,' Mr Hardy said, his voice tinged with pride and affection. There was a broad smile on his face as he leaned over and gave the woman a reassuring peck on the cheek.

John stood stock-still. He frowned at his father.

'Didn't I say he should have told the boy beforehand?' Ernie mumbled.

'Shh!' Walter warned again. He took a long sip from his glass.

But Mandy agreed with Ernie. If your father suddenly got engaged, you'd want to be the first to know. 'This isn't the kind of Easter surprise I'd like!' she whispered to James. She felt sorry for John, standing there by his suitcase.

'John, this isn't like you,' Mr Hardy said. The smile had vanished from his face.

Instead of saying hello to the fair-haired woman, as his father wanted, John deliberately turned aside and made a great show of having spotted Mandy and James. He greeted them like long-lost friends. 'Hey!' He waved, and strode across. 'Just the people I wanted to see!'

'I don't think!' Ernie muttered.

'John!' Julian Hardy called, obviously annoyed.

'Hello, John,' Mandy stammered. 'How was school?'

'Fine, thanks. I wanted to talk to you about a project I have to do this holiday.' Still he ignored his father and poor Sara, who between them came out and struggled towards the door with the

'Nay, the poor chap would melt by the fire!' Walter put in. He grinned at James. 'Young sir, you should never have gone to this trouble for old Ernie and me, you know!'

'Hey, hey, I'm not so old!' Ernie grumbled. He winked at Mandy. 'I reckon you've been into Walton and paid a visit to Harry Cecil's posh shop. He's not cheap, I'm told. You shouldn't have, like Walter says.'

His face set in a frown, but Mandy could tell he was pleased. She and James turned to leave, but Walter half stood up from his bench and stopped them.

'Hang on a minute! What's this?'

A low, dark green car sped down the high street, past the post office. It drew into the pub carpark and the engine died.

'It's the boss!' Ernie said, meaning Mr Hardy, the pub landlord. He called a warning to the bar staff inside. 'Look lively! He's back!'

They heard empty glasses clink and rattle as the staff quickly removed them from view.

'Didn't he go over to fetch his boy earlier this afternoon?' Walter asked. He turned to James. 'It seems to me young John Hardy is in for a surprise when he goes inside!'

John had just got out of his father's car. He
looked up at the pub, at the room where he lived
with his father during the holidays. During term
time he lived seventy or eighty kilometres away at
Grange School in the Lake District.

James frowned, then turned to Mandy. 'Didn't
his dad tell him about Sara?'

'Shh!' Walter warned.

Mandy widened her eyes and shook her head.
John's dad, Julian, had announced his
engagement just a week ago. His fiancée was one
of the women who helped behind the bar.

'Just look at that whacking great suitcase,' Ernie
pointed out. 'What's he got in there, the kitchen
sink?'

Mandy saw Mr Hardy lift a case out of the boot.
He let it thump heavily to the ground.

It was all too easy to forget about John Hardy
when he was away at school. Mandy had known
him all her life, yet never known him. That was
the peculiar thing. He was eleven, the same age
as James, and he was even born in the same week
at Walton Maternity Hospital. He was a small,
neat, ordinary-looking boy, with dark, wavy hair
that seemed to make his face rounder and a bit
too goody-goody. It was the sort of hair that always

stayed in place. He was never untidy, never hot, never running; always walking in his cool, collected manner. He looked more grown-up than eleven, but Mandy never thought he looked very happy.

'Come on, John,' his father said, leaving the suitcase where it was. He headed for the front door with eager steps. 'Leave that. I've got some news for you, and there's someone inside I want you to meet.' He smiled and went on ahead.

Mandy saw John hesitate. He was wearing a light Aran sweater and jeans. His white sports shoes looked brand-new, but somehow he looked as if he was in his Sunday best. Then Sara came to the door to greet them both. She looked nervous as she stood there waiting.

Ernie grunted, but Walter leaned across and jabbed him with his elbow. 'I'm saying nothing!' Ernie protested. But Mandy thought his sour look said plenty.

They watched uneasily as Sara clasped he hands in front of her.

'John, this is Sara,' Mr Hardy said, his voi tinged with pride and affection. There was a bro smile on his face as he leaned over and gave woman a reassuring peck on the cheek.

John stood stock-still. He frowned at his father.

'Didn't I say he should have told the boy beforehand?' Ernie mumbled.

'Shh!' Walter warned again. He took a long sip from his glass.

But Mandy agreed with Ernie. If your father suddenly got engaged, you'd want to be the first to know. 'This isn't the kind of Easter surprise I'd like!' she whispered to James. She felt sorry for John, standing there by his suitcase.

'John, this isn't like you,' Mr Hardy said. The smile had vanished from his face.

Instead of saying hello to the fair-haired woman, ᵆs his father wanted, John deliberately turned ᵘide and made a great show of having spotted ᵘndy and James. He greeted them like long-lost ᵘnds. 'Hey!' He waved, and strode across. 'Just ᵖeople I wanted to see!'

ᵒn't think!' Ernie muttered.

ᵘn!' Julian Hardy called, obviously annoyed.

ᵒ, John,' Mandy stammered. 'How was

ᵉ   ᵗhanks. I wanted to talk to you about a
ᵈ   ᵃave to do this holiday.' Still he ignored
ʰe   ᵈd poor Sara, who between them came
       ᵘggled towards the door with the

outsize suitcase. 'This project has to do with animals,' John explained. But his warm tone seemed forced. 'I have to choose an animal and study it in its natural habitat. You know all about animals, don't you, Mandy? You must do; you live at the vets' place.'

Mandy swallowed hard and glanced at James. John Hardy seemed to have the habit of coolly ignoring everyone except the person he wanted to speak to. For the moment, that was her. 'What kind of animal?' she said, blushing at his rudeness.

'That's what I want to talk to you about,' John began. But before he could get any further, his father reached the door. Mr Hardy had to stoop to enter the porch. Mandy noticed that he had the same wavy hair as his son, but a thinner face, and there was a scattering of grey at the temples. He turned to whisper a word to Sara, who nodded, smiled emptily, then went inside once more.

'John!' Mr Hardy said in a stern voice. 'Come here!'

His son pursed his lips. 'I'll come and see you at Animal Ark soon,' he told Mandy. Then he obeyed his father.

'I said it meant trouble!' Ernie warned.

Mandy saw Walter lean over and carefully, deliberately, step on his toe.

'Ouch!' Ernie yelled.

Julian Hardy took John off to a far corner of the carpark to give him a good dressing-down for his rudeness to Sara.

Mandy heard his raised voice. She saw John duck his head and take a step back.

'Well, I'm off home now,' James said quickly, and shot off down the road.

'Bye!' Mandy waved. She didn't like rows either, but somehow she felt rooted to the spot, there outside the Fox and Goose. Soon Mr Hardy lowered his voice and led John out of sight, round the back of the pub. 'Why did John behave like that?' she asked Walter and Ernie.

'Refuse to say hello to Sara, you mean?' Walter shrugged. 'It looks like it was too much to cope with. The poor lad's had his dad to himself all these years.'

'He's not usually like that,' Mandy agreed. Just the opposite. Whenever she'd seen him before, John was always annoyingly polite. 'But he'll soon find out that Sara's OK. I like her. She calls in at Animal Ark sometimes to chat with my mum. She's just moved up to Welford from Sheffield.'

'OK or not, John doesn't want to know,' Ernie pointed out.

'But she even looks great,' Mandy objected. Sara wore fashionable, bright clothes, and looked young for her age. Mandy's mother and Sara had been at school together.

'Give him time!' Walter stood up. 'It'll sort itself out.' He picked up the chocolate frog from the bench beside him and strolled the short distance to his own cottage.

Ernie gave a grimace. 'Maybe.' He followed slowly after Walter. 'Then again, maybe not.'

Mandy stood for a while in the empty porch. *Poor John,* she said to herself. *It can't be easy coming home to find everything has suddenly changed.*

She wasn't surprised when, just seconds later, a side door flew open and John Hardy burst out. His father shouted after him, but the boy took no notice.

He ran through the walled garden at the back of the pub. He flung open the gate and began to leap, then stumble, up the steep hill. He cut across one field, vaulted a low stone wall and kept on running. Mandy had glimpsed his face as he came out. It was crumpled and tear-stained. John looked desperate.

Where can he run to? Mandy wondered. He was bolting, just like a rabbit. She watched him charge wildly up the hill into the middle of nowhere.

Three

'*Run, rabbit, run, rabbit, run, run, run.*
Here comes the farmer with his gun, gun, gun!'

Mr Hope's rich baritone voice rang out through the empty surgery.

'*He'll get by without his rabbit pie,*
So run, rabbit, run, rabbit, run, run, run!'

'Very nice,' Jean Knox commented, peering into the treatment room. She had just arrived at Animal Ark. 'Now, where did I put that appointment book?' She searched high and low behind the reception desk. 'I don't know, I'd forget my head if it were loose!'

Mandy grinned at her dad, then went through and put her hands straight on the big red diary lying on the desk. 'Here it is!'

Their grey-haired receptionist gave a surprised gasp. 'Oh, thank you, Mandy dear. What would I do without you?' Jean, flustered as usual, began the search for her car keys. 'Now *where* did I put those keys?' she muttered.

'In your coat pocket?' Mandy suggested.

'Ah yes, how clever!' She felt in her pocket and gave a relieved sigh.

Jean went back to reception, clutching her keys, searching for her glasses, which hung as usual on a chain round her neck.

Mandy giggled. 'Dad, do you need me?' she asked. It was the first proper day of her school holiday, a Monday morning, and she had great plans. She and James wanted to go bird-watching by the river. He'd recently seen a kingfisher wing its way under the low stone arch of the old bridge, and they wanted to spot it together.

'Twitching, is it?' Dad said, locking the door of the drugs cupboard and looking at his watch. 'Twitching' was his name for crouching in the undergrowth with a pair of binoculars, waiting for the kingfisher to show up.

'I've got to feed the rabbits first,' she announced. 'Then maybe we'll go twitching. James said he'd ring me.'

She went out into the garden, armed with the bag of dried oats and other cereal for Flopsy, Mopsy and Cottontail. She thought of scatter-brained Jean, whom she often felt like teasing. 'Now, *where* did I put those rabbits?' she said, teetering on the doorstep.

Dad laughed and wandered out after her. The grass was dewy in the cool morning air as they headed for the hutch at the bottom of the garden.

Mandy greeted her three rabbits and quietly set about clearing the cage of the old bedding, while Dad set first Flopsy, then Mopsy, then Cottontail out in the long wire run where they exercised. Big, sleek, black and white rabbits, they sat in the sun and combed their whiskers.

'Dad, I was wondering. How do you think they'd feel if I changed their names?' she asked. She laid fresh straw in the clean cage. *You grow out of names,* she thought. Now she preferred Button and Barney, and perhaps Benji in honour of James's cat, who had died. The old names seemed a little childish.

'Hmm,' Dad said thoughtfully. 'On the whole, I think they'd probably prefer to stay the same.'

'You're probably right,' she agreed. 'Flopsy, Mopsy and Cottontail is what they've always been.'

Dad helped Mandy by tying a tight knot in the top of the bag of used straw and droppings. 'Good for you,' he said.

She smiled.

'Mandy, you've got a visitor!' Mrs Hope called from inside the house. Her long, red hair was framed in the doorway, and shone bright in the morning sun. 'It's John Hardy!'

'Uh-oh!' Mandy stood up. She'd managed to forget the uncomfortable scene at the Fox and Goose when John had snubbed his father's new fiancée. Now she remembered that he'd promised to call in at Animal Ark.

'Trouble?' Dad asked.

'Not really. I'd better go in and see, though.' She left her father to finish tidying up in the garden and traipsed indoors. Her mum had vanished somewhere upstairs, so she stood face to face with John in the empty kitchen.

'Hello, Mandy,' he said. He was calm and matter-of-fact again, but she still had a clear memory of his tear-stained face as he ran up the hill. He'd come today equipped with camera, notebook and binoculars, and stood looking annoyingly neat and studious. He forgot to smile when he greeted her.

'Hi.' Her own friendly smile faltered. Why did she feel as if she'd just walked into an exam room? Her stomach knotted as she felt him sum up her and her surroundings. She kicked her dad's scruffy slippers out of sight under the table.

'Animals!' John Hardy announced. 'What sort do you suggest?' He looked round the kitchen as if a suitable specimen might suddenly appear.

'Well, there's a lot to choose from at this time of year. If you just look around for something to study, there's—'

'Before you go on, don't say tadpoles, whatever you do!' John interrupted. 'Everyone suggests tadpoles, and they're so boring!'

'Oh, but they're not!' Mandy began. 'Their life cycle is amazing!' Then she stopped. She saw his mind was set against them.

'Anyway, that's kid's stuff,' John said. 'No, I want

to study something that's nice to look at, not disgusting, like tadpoles. Something I can take good pictures of!' He tapped his camera, slung on a strap round his neck. It had levers and lenses and buttons all over the place. This was no seaside holiday camera. 'Well?' John prompted. He stood with his feet wide apart on the Hopes' flagged kitchen floor.

She looked to the beamed ceiling for inspiration, then her gaze swept round the room. There on a shelf on the pine dresser sat her Easter present for Lydia Fawcett, all done up in its bright yellow bow. 'Rabbits!' she said suddenly.

'Rabbits?' John looked suspicious. 'Don't they just sit there and eat lettuce?'

'No, they're brilliant creatures to study. I've been reading up about them. For instance, their warrens are amazing! They meet in big underground chambers, held up with tree roots, with air-conditioning and everything!'

'Air-conditioning?'

'Yes, they build their runs facing away from the wind for warmth, but they connect them up with small runs that open on to the fresh air. Of course, they sleep close together for warmth.'

'How do you know all this?' John was still frowning, but the bit about air-conditioning seemed to have roused his interest. He strode to the window to look out down the lane.

'You won't see any down there,' Mandy explained. 'There are too many trees. And rabbits like high ground. Hillsides, where the wind can carry sound, the ground is dry, and they can smell danger.'

'How do you *know*?' John insisted.

'Like I said, I just sat down last night and read a book,' she confessed, feeling herself go red. She'd taken it down from the shelf in the surgery. 'It's over there on the dresser. I'll ask my dad if you can borrow it, if you like.'

The idea of a textbook also appealed to John, as Mandy guessed it would. He was a boy who liked to study. '*The Private Life of the Rabbit* by R.M. Lockley,' he read out loud as he picked up the heavy volume. 'Have you read it all?'

'No, but it's best to study the rabbits out in the wild before you go in for too much reading. Your project will be much better if you begin with a kind of diary of their habits.' Actually, Mandy was keen to get John Hardy to make up his mind. Then she thought she could take him up to the Celtic

cross on the moorside, to one of the High Cross
fields. At the same time she would deliver the
chocolate bunny to Lydia. 'You know; begin with
a chapter called "Rabbit Habits", or something
like that!' she said eagerly.

No smile appeared in response, to crack the
earnest expression on John's face. 'I suppose
you're right. I've got thirty-six exposures on this
film. Colour. Fast speed. High definition.' He
paused again. 'You're sure rabbits are interesting
enough?'

'If you've got enough patience to study them –
yes!' Mandy grabbed the present from the shelf.
'I know just the place!' she insisted. 'Ready?'

He nodded, and Mandy called up to her mum.
She was anxious to set off. 'Won't be long! I'm
just taking John up to High Cross!'

'OK!' Mrs Hope's voice floated downstairs.
'Oh, Mandy, James Hunter phoned while you
were busy in the surgery. I said you'd ring
him!'

'Thanks. I'll do it when I get back.' She
scrambled into her jacket, which hung from a
hook on the wall, and dashed out of the house.

At least she'd got John Hardy sorted out with a
school project. She breathed in deeply and

marched alongside him up the lane.

They trekked by the public footpath across the fields beside Brandon Gill's pig farm. Mandy paused to pick up a stick and give Nelson, the great black and white boar, a quick backscratch. Nelson grunted contentedly and trampled the earth.

John wrinkled his nose. 'I'm glad you suggested rabbits, not pigs,' he said.

Mandy's eyebrows shot up. John Hardy had nearly made a joke. In fact, he seemed to be unwinding as they walked. The wind had even ruffled his hair. There was colour in his cheeks, and his dark eyes had come alive. They darted from hedgerow to bramble thicket, searching for rabbits.

It must be difficult for him, she thought again, *trying to settle in at home, with Sara there so much of the time.* Mandy knew better than to mention Sara's name outright, or to seem too curious. Walter Pickard was right; John would need time to get used to the new situation.

As he relaxed, John began to chat about the Celtic cross landmark way up on the hill, past Beacon House. He knew its history and how it had come to be there. Mandy noticed he didn't vary his pace, but strode on like a man with a mission. Most kids she knew would stop to poke round in ditches or to climb a tempting tree. But John Hardy set his face straight ahead and made it a route march. Soon they'd passed the grand iron gates of Beacon House, the Parker Smythe place, and then the entrance to Upper Welford Hall. Mandy had to drag John to a halt by the old five-barred gate that marked the entrance to High Cross Farm.

'Hang on a sec!' she gasped. 'We're here! Let me just pop in and ask Lydia if we can use her fields to scout around for rabbits. And I want to give her this.' She held up the cellophane package.

'Hmm . . .' John frowned. 'I'll wait here and keep a lookout!' He stood bolt upright, binoculars poised.

Mandy dashed inside. She found Lydia in the barn, tending to her beloved goats. Dressed in her oldest wellingtons and her tattered brown work jacket, she was mucking out the stalls and turning each of her goats out to graze in the spring pasture. Houdini, the most mischievous of all, stood in his stall and snickered at Mandy as she approached.

'Hello, Houdini!' Mandy circled her arms about his neck and hugged him. Houdini bared his teeth. His hooves clattered against the wooden door. 'Steady, boy!' She backed off and greeted Lydia. 'Happy Easter!' she said shyly, handing over the small present.

'What's this?' A smile lit up Lydia's face, so that it wrinkled like a shiny old apple. 'Why it's a little bunny rabbit; how clever!' She unwrapped the chocolate like a child at Christmas, then she perched the rabbit gleefully in the palm of her hand.

In an instant, Houdini's bony head darted forward, and he wrapped his rubbery lips round the too-tempting gift. Gulp! Swallow! Lick! It was gone.

'Oh!' Lydia cried out, her face crumpling. Then she laughed. 'Oh, Houdini!'

Mandy joined in the laughter. 'He must have thought it was for him!'

'Tut!' Lydia clicked her tongue. 'His manners are appalling, and he's old enough to know better!' With a good-natured pat of the goat's neck, she unbolted the door and led him out into the farmyard. 'I bet it tasted first class, didn't it, boy?' she grumbled. 'And I'm sure you'd like to say a big thank you to Mandy here!'

Houdini tossed his head and trotted on.

'Talking of rabbits . . .' Mandy said as she spied John Hardy waiting patiently by the gate.

'Were we?' Lydia shot Mandy a quick glance. 'Oh, yes, rabbits . . . chocolate . . . oh, Houdini . . . oh dear!' She chortled and led him on, out to the near pasture. 'Rabbits, yes. Well, we have plenty of them round here, of course.' She let Houdini loose in the field, closed the gate, and leaned forward against the top bar. She gestured towards the field full of fresh dandelions, willowherb and yellow coltsfoot. 'Not in here, of course. The little nuisances know to keep off when the goats are about. No, the sly things keep their distance. But if you go up to the far pasture, the one beyond the house, that field will be alive with them. You can't move up there without tripping over a rabbit hole!'

As Lydia grumbled on, Mandy lost heart. It really did seem that even gentle Lydia saw rabbits as pests. In that case she might not be keen to let a stranger from the village begin his study on one of her fields.

'Mind you, I have to admit that they're bonny little things.' She leaned both elbows on the gate and clasped her broad hands. 'And friendly, so long as you keep your distance; and who can blame them? Many a time I go up there in the evening and watch them come out to feed. They're quite delightful!' She laughed and brought herself up short. 'We farmers aren't supposed to have a soft spot for rabbits, I suppose!'

'But you wouldn't mind if a friend of mine came up to take pictures and make notes, would you?' Mandy seized her chance. 'He has to do some work on rabbits for a school project. I said I thought it would be OK.'

Lydia stood upright and glanced in John's direction. 'That's not young James Hunter, is it?' She screwed up her eyes and raised one hand to shield them from the sun.

'No, it's John Hardy from the Fox and Goose.'

Lydia nodded, then looked up at the sun. 'Time I was getting on with the cheese-making,' she said. 'You know there's no peace for the wicked!' She glanced again at the lonely figure by the gate. 'Tell your friend he's welcome. And to call in at the house for a cup of tea whenever he has the time!'

Mandy thanked her and ran back to John. Soon they were up on Lydia's far pasture and he was crouched down behind the rain-blackened stone wall, camera at the ready. One or two rabbits roamed the far side of the field. He stood up suddenly. They stood stork-still, then vanished down separate holes as he clicked the shutter.

'Missed!' he muttered.

'See!' Mandy told him. 'Didn't I say they were clever? They have fantastic hearing!'

John nodded, then scanned the rough, empty field. 'I'll wait,' he insisted. This time he put his binoculars to his eyes and trained them on the grass.

'It's probably a bit late for rabbits by now,' Mandy said. 'But they do like the sun, so maybe a few will come back for a snack!'

'I'll wait,' he said again, crouching down still as a statue. 'You know, I think your idea about rabbits was good,' he admitted, giving Mandy a brief smile. 'Thanks.' And he settled down to watch.

It was the start of a long, patient campaign by the boy from the pub.

A short time later, Mandy left John to go home and phone James. Then her day was busy. First she went bird-watching. After lunch she helped in the surgery, then she popped into Lilac Cottage to visit her grandparents. But when she cycled back up to High Cross after tea, John Hardy was still there, crouched behind a wall. He hadn't moved all day. All round him, scattered on the grass, lay white sheets of paper.

Mandy left her bike at the main gate and walked across.

'Hush!' he warned. The rabbits were coming out in their hordes as dusk approached. This was their liveliest time of day.

Quietly Mandy crouched beside him. Many of the sheets were covered in tiny writing; scrawled notes about sightings and the position of rabbit burrows. Sometimes John had stopped to sketch a rabbit in fine pencil. She picked up one of these drawings and found it beautifully done. The rabbit's eyes shone like blackcurrants out of its soft, furry face. The ears stood straight, paler on the inside, with black, pointed tips. 'This is good!' Mandy exclaimed. 'I never knew you could draw!'

'You never asked!' John whispered. 'Art is one of my favourite subjects at school. Now quiet, please, or you'll scare them off.'

They watched as more rabbits popped out of their holes, then stopped and sniffed the air. They rocked forwards on to their short front legs and lazily hopped towards a tender shoot of cowslip or dandelion. Their ears twitched and they sniffed the air, but they grazed happily enough. The large male rabbits stayed at the centre of the warren, pushing the smaller yearlings to the outskirts. The young ones had to look out for foxes, weasels, or even the vicious rooks that sat high in the ash trees and cawed.

After a day on duty, John seemed to have learned a lot about studying rabbits. He'd taken off his white sweater, realising that his dark blue T-shirt made him stand out less. He moved smoothly, and didn't jerk when he raised his head above the wall to take more photographs. This time the rabbits' ears still twitched in response, but they carried on feeding, untroubled.

'Well done!' Mandy whispered.

John crouched back down and nodded. 'Thanks. I've had a great time!' He confessed it awkwardly, blushing. The sun had brought up the freckles in his dark skin. 'Now I'd like to find a field with an old warren in it; one that's not used any more. I want to explore how the rabbits make their burrows.'

'How about tomorrow?' Mandy suggested. 'You must be starving hungry. And doesn't your dad need to know where you are?'

Sharply John shook his head. 'He doesn't care.' His voice was flat. Carefully he unscrewed the big lens from his camera and packed it into its case.

'Oh, I'm sure he does!' Mandy began.

But John ignored her. 'So where can I find an *old* warren?' he insisted.

She thought hard. 'Let's go and ask Lydia,' she suggested. She could see that this would be the first of many visits this Easter to High Cross and the rabbit fields. John had taken to her idea better than she expected. What's more, it would keep him busy, and well out of the way of Sara and his dad. No wonder he seemed keen.

'You should be a wildlife artist,' she told him as she helped pack away the sketches. 'I never thought you'd be so interested in animals!'

'You never asked!' he said again.

Mandy stared at him. This time she knew it was a joke. She checked his dark brown eyes; they were sparkling. 'Come on, let's go,' she said. They ran down to the farm together, to a cup of hot tea and Lydia's home-made scones.

Four

'Mandy, James phoned again!' Jean Knox called from the surgery.

Mandy had just got back from High Cross. It was the second week of the Easter holiday; every day the weather grew warmer, the trees greener.

'Or was it John Hardy?' Jean's puzzled voice quavered. 'Oh dear, which one was it?'

Mandy went into reception. She felt flushed from the sun, and tired after the day's explorations. 'It can't have been John,' she exclaimed. 'I just left him outside the Fox and Goose.'

'Oh well, it was James, then,' Jean decided. She

was searching for something in a drawer as usual. 'Now where did I put that—'

'Appointment book?' Mandy broke in.

'Yes, how did you know? . . . Oh, thank you, dear!' Jean smiled brightly. 'Yes, now I come to think of it, it must have been James. He told me he was just back from visiting his aunt and uncle in London, and he wondered if you wanted to play tennis.'

'Great, thanks.' Mandy had dashed back to Animal Ark to do her cleaning chores, but she broke off to pick up the phone and ring her friend. 'Sorry, James, I've just been so busy all day. Did you have a nice couple of days in London?'

'It was OK, thanks. What have you been up to?'

'I've been busy helping on John's school project. We're making a detailed study of the female rabbits now, and their young. John's numbered all the burrows with kittens, and . . .'

'Kittens?'

She heard James's voice sounding confused. 'The baby rabbits. They're called kittens. The females are called does. It says so in this book we've got, *The Private Life of the Rabbit* by R.M. Lockley.'

'Oh.' Now James sounded distant and bored.

'Anyway, we've noticed that most of the litters have five kittens. Some have six. And when the yearlings are strong enough, they move off to form new warrens because the old one gets over-crowded with the new babies. They start all over again on fresh ground.' She rattled on.

'Fancy a game of tennis tonight, then?' James asked in an offhand way.

Mandy thought ahead. She hated to turn him down. After all, he was her best friend, and they always tried to arrange to do things together. 'Oh, James, I'm sorry, I can't! I'm going back over to John's to help him choose some photos for his project. I promised!' Then she hit on an answer. 'How about tomorrow morning?' she asked. 'Meet at my house at about ten? I'll have to dig out my racket from somewhere, and see you then.'

'Fine,' came James's quick reply. 'Bye.' The phone clicked and the line went dead.

Jean nodded her approval. 'Good for you. He rang earlier, but you always seem to be out.'

Mandy sighed. 'I know. Anyway, I must get a move on. I said to John I'd be back at his place by six-thirty!' She swept round the treatment rooms like a whirlwind with her disinfected cloths and hot mop and bucket. In the residential unit at the back of the surgery, she spoke nicely to the Persian cat who'd just been spayed. Then she went out briskly to clean and feed her own rabbits. It was time to go. 'See you later!' she called to whoever was inside the house to hear.

'Don't forget to pop in and see your gran sometime soon,' her dad said. He was sitting with his feet up in the lounge. 'She tells me she hasn't set eyes on you for ages!'

'OK, I'll call in later! Got to dash!' Mandy scrambled free of the house and cycled off up the lane. She was eager to see how John's latest batch of photos had turned out. He'd used his zoom lens to take close-ups of the babies as they emerged from the burrows for the first time. They looked like small fawn balls of spun sugar, with enormous eyes and ears.

She propped her bike against the side wall of the pub and nipped in through the garden. She knocked at the door, then went quickly up the back stairs to John's room. It was a low, old house with thick stone walls and small windows. There was a landing halfway up the stairs with a red and blue stained-glass window which overlooked the garden. The old wooden boards creaked as she went on upstairs, and the dark corridor to John's room sloped at an odd angle, like a gangway on a ferry. She knocked loud and clear on the old panelled door.

'Come in!' John looked up excitedly as Mandy opened it. 'The photos have arrived!'

'I can see that!' she laughed. John sat amongst dozens of colour pictures of the rabbits on the far pasture at High Cross. They were scattered across the red carpet, and some were pinned crookedly to his bedroom walls. More scribbled notes lay across the desk, and his sketches decorated the front of the wardrobe, the door

into his bathroom, and even inside the bathroom itself. 'It's worse than *my* room, and that's saying something!' Mandy liked to stick pictures of all her favourite animals on the walls at home, but at least she put them on straight and arranged them neatly. John had simply slapped these on anyhow, and she was surprised because he seemed so tidy in other ways.

'They're the best yet!' he announced. He held up a large, glossy photo to the light and studied it. 'See, I got the angle just right on this one, and the focus is really sharp. The doe is sitting upright at the entrance to the burrow. See, even her whiskers have come out clearly!'

Mandy admired the photos. 'They're really good, John. It's going to be difficult to choose the best.' She knelt down on the floor beside him, but then she glanced at her hands and saw that they needed a wash. 'Hang on, I'll just have to go and wash my hands,' she told him. She went through into the small white bathroom.

'I'll nip down and get us some juice.' John managed to tear himself away from his precious pictures.

Mandy heard the bedroom door open and close. She took her time running the water, soaping her hands and gazing round at John's beautiful sketches of rabbits. His pictures showed their gracefulness; the thing she most loved about them herself. He really was a good artist, she thought. 'Bunnies in the bathroom!' she said to herself with a funny little smile.

She dried her hands. John was taking a long time fetching the drinks. She crossed the bedroom floor, picking her way between the photos. Then she peered out into the long, crooked corridor.

'Hi!' A bright, pleasant voice caught her by surprise.

'Oh, hi!' Mandy recognised the golden hair and neat, slim figure of Julian Hardy's fiancée, Sara. She was dressed in a loose, silky, white shirt and a long blue skirt, with open sandals and bare legs. She wore her long hair swept up casually on top of her head, but strands had escaped and caught in her dangling gold earrings. Her face had tanned in the sun, emphasising her wide, light grey eyes. 'I'm looking for John,' Mandy explained, feeling out of place.

'I saw him go downstairs not long ago.' Sara smiled. 'I'm Sara Lawson. I'm engaged to John's dad.'

'I know.' Mandy saw the diamond engagement

ring on her left hand. She blushed. John really would have to get used to the new situation, like it or not. She thought again that Sara seemed friendly and pretty.

'I'm afraid John and I haven't hit it off yet,' she confessed. She seemed to want to talk to someone. 'Things have been a bit tense since he came back from school. He's out studying those rabbits all the time, or else he just stays in his room and avoids me.' She gave an embarrassed little laugh. 'I don't think he likes me much!'

'Oh, he's never said that!' Mandy protested. She felt her clean palms go hot and sticky again. She didn't fancy being caught up in this problem; it seemed too big for her to do anything about.

'Why, what has he said?' Sara stood facing Mandy in the corridor, a serious look on her face.

'Nothing. He never mentions you.' Mandy had spent hours with John during this last week, while James had been away. They'd braved the wind, rain and sunshine up on the fields at High Cross. She'd crouched behind thick tree trunks with him in the hour before dawn, and returned at dusk to study the rabbits. But he'd never once talked about his family or home.

Sara nodded. 'Exactly. He treats me as if I'm invisible. He seems to think that I'll just vanish, I'm sure he does!' She glanced into his room at the sketches on the walls. 'He's got talent though. You have to say that for him.'

'Yes!' Glad to change the subject, Mandy agreed. 'I think he should be a wildlife artist, or a photographer!'

Raised voices from the garden filtered through the open window. Mandy paused and checked Sara's worried expression. They both recognised another row brewing between Julian Hardy and his son.

'And another thing; just when are you going to tidy up that room of yours?' Mr Hardy demanded. His voice came from the kitchen downstairs. 'It's a complete mess in there. You can't expect Sara or me to go in and tidy up after you, if you leave it in that sort of state!'

There was no reply. Mandy heard a fridge door slam shut.

'John, I'm talking to you! I said, when are you going to clean up all that mess? Scraps of paper and drawings everywhere!'

'It's for my school project.' John sounded slow and sulky. 'I've got to get it finished.'

'But you don't have to clutter the whole place up!' Mr Hardy's voice faded, then John appeared from the kitchen at the foot of the stairs. He began to trail up them, a glass of orange juice in each hand. 'Are you listening to me, or am I just wasting my breath?' His father pursued him into the hallway.

Sara took a deep breath and leaned over the banister. 'Leave him alone now, Julian,' she called out. 'I'm sure he'll tidy up when he's finished his project!'

Mandy felt she could have heard a pin drop. John looked up at Sara with a blank expression. Julian stood, taken aback, hands on hips, one foot on the bottom step.

'And you should see his sketches of those rabbits! They're brilliant!' Sara tried to smooth things out.

There was another tense silence. Then John snapped. His face crumpled. 'Who asked you?' he demanded. 'Who said you could go in my room and snoop around?'

Suddenly he turned and tripped. Mandy watched as the two full glasses tipped against the white wall. The orange liquid splashed against it and trickled down. John stared at it in dismay.

'John!' His father yelled out a warning, but it was too late.

Sara put one hand over her mouth and stepped quickly back.

But John dived downstairs with a weird cry. He rushed past his father and fled, head down, straight out through the kitchen, across the garden into the main street. Mandy raced after him.

'Nay,' Ernie Bell advised. He stopped her short by putting out a hand from his position on the bench in the front porch. 'Leave him be. There's enough trouble round here as it is. Don't you go adding to it.'

Mandy glanced down at Ernie, her eyes watering, her heart pounding. She saw John disappear over a stile into the fields behind the McFarlanes' post office.

Ernie was right; she was out of her depth. Sadly she went home in the fading light.

John came over to Animal Ark early next morning. He was dressed in a green zip-up jacket, camera at the ready. His face gave nothing away as Mandy went to answer the door. 'Hi, I thought we could get the bus over to Walton today, before we go up to High Cross.' He waited for her to collect her thoughts. 'There's a book I want to get from the library.'

Mandy glanced at her watch. It was half-past nine. Mrs Hope and Simon were busy in the surgery. Her father was out on his rounds. There was no chance of a lift into town, and she knew that John didn't have a bike. 'I'll just ask Jean what time the next bus goes,' she told him. 'Hang on here a minute.'

Though he looked the same as usual, spruced up and calm, Mandy thought he sounded tense, and she spotted a pleading look behind his eyes, as if he needed her company today of all days. She opened the door into reception, to a chorus of growls, barks and miaows. 'Jean, when's the next bus into Walton?' She leaned across the counter and shouted over the noise.

Jean checked her watch. 'In ten minutes. From the post office.'

'We'll just make it. Thanks!' Mandy made as if to sprint off.

'Mandy!' Jean called.

'See you later. Tell Mum I've gone into town, will you, please?' She shot off back into the house, to find John answering the front door to James Hunter.

James stood on the doorstep, tennis bag in one hand. He wore his blue and red track suit and white tennis shoes. He looked up at John. 'Is Mandy in?' he stammered.

'James!' she gasped. She dashed up from behind. 'Oh no, I forgot!' Both boys stared at her. 'I mean, I didn't exactly forget! Anyway, you're early!' She felt her stomach tilt. What should she do now?

'It's all right, never mind.' James stood there, two steps down in the breezy morning air. 'I should have rung you up to check it was still OK.' He stopped, lost for words.

John stood in the hall with a slight frown creasing his smooth forehead. Then he caught sight of Jean Knox, following Mandy through from the surgery.

'James, can we just change our plan a bit?' Mandy asked. She felt flustered. 'Why don't we all slip over to town together, then fit in a game of tennis?'

'No thanks. I'd rather go on down to the tennis-courts by myself,' James said quietly. He turned and wandered off up the drive. 'I'll find someone to play with, no problem. See you later.'

John blinked at Mandy. 'Is it my fault?' he asked.

'No, of course not; it's not your fault.' Mandy's stomach still hadn't regained its balance. She felt churned up inside.

'Mandy?' Jean said quietly. She came up close. 'John, why don't you go ahead to the bus stop?' she suggested in a firm but kindly voice. 'And perhaps Mandy will join you later.'

A blush flooded across John's face, but he nodded and went off nonetheless. Jean closed the door after him and put an arm around Mandy's shoulder. Then she led her into the kitchen.

'I never meant to do that to James!' Mandy said. She felt helpless, and a kind of hot guilt was creeping up her neck. She put up her hand to hide it.

'No, I'm sure you didn't.' Jean put on the kettle. She seemed to know exactly where everything was at this moment; the switch, the tea-bags, her glasses. She sounded calm and looked gently at Mandy. 'But if you were James and thought that someone had come along and stepped into your shoes, how do you think you would feel?'

'Lousy,' Mandy admitted. 'But it won't be for long. John has to go back to school next week, and he has to finish that rabbit project. I'm just lending a hand!'

'Yes.' Jean gazed steadily at her. 'You know, it puts me in mind of something that happened to me when I was eight; and that's well over fifty years ago now!' She settled at the table opposite Mandy and seemed to look down a long corridor into the past. 'It was summer, I remember, and I'd been on holiday to Blackpool. I brought a stick of pink rock back for my best friend. She was called Margaret; Margaret Taylor. We were like two peas in a pod.

'Well, I went up to her back garden with the stick of rock the minute we got home. She was playing there with a girl who lived down the street; Susan Turnbull. A girl with beautiful blonde plaits. Margaret looked at me across her garden fence. Her nose went up in the air. "I don't want your smelly stick of rock!" she told me. And she turned back to play with Susan. Well, sometimes we can all be nasty and spiteful like that, I know, but it was worse than any smack or telling off I'd had in my entire life, I can tell you.'

'And you were best friends?' Mandy asked. Her throat felt dry and narrow. Did it look as if she'd just done something similar to James?

'Yes. That's probably what put me in mind of you and James.' Jean stopped to sip her tea.

'And did you ever play with her again after that?' Mandy hoped the story would have a happy ending.

'I expect so. Yes, of course I did. Next day she was my best friend again, no doubt. And I suppose we were even nasty to Susan Turnbull on occasions. She was a big-headed girl because her father owned a chemists' shop and drove a Morris Oxford; a big black car,' Jean explained. Then she sighed. 'But I never forgot that stick of rock!'

Mandy jumped up from the table, her mind made up. 'Thanks, Jean!' she said.

'Why, where are you going?'

'To find my tennis racket!' Mandy said.

'It's under the counter in the surgery,' Jean told her with a smile. 'I noticed it lurking there yesterday. And there's a new set of balls and your tennis shoes. I expect your track suit's up in your wardrobe drawer!'

Mandy nearly dropped through the floor with shock. She stared at Jean. 'Thanks!' she stammered again.

'Now, *where* did I put my glasses?' Jean

mumbled. She carried the empty mugs to the sink. 'I'm sure I put them somewhere sensible . . .'

'Round your neck!' Mandy yelled. She was through the door, racket in hand, shoes hooked by their laces round her own neck. She dashed up the drive. 'See you later, Jean!'

James beat her seven-five, six-four, even though she was trying really hard to win.

After the game, they went straight back to Mandy's house for a sandwich lunch.

'Sorry about this morning,' Mandy mumbled, her mouth full of crusty french bread. 'It's just that I was pretty worried about John. Things aren't any better for him at home. In fact, I think they're worse. He can't seem to get over the shock of his dad getting engaged.' She told James about her visit the previous evening.

'Maybe he's jealous?' James said thoughtfully. 'Of Sara, I mean.'

'But she's really nice. He hasn't even given her a chance!'

'You don't when you're jealous, do you?'

Mandy stopped chewing and sighed. 'You're right. Anyway, I am sorry!' she repeated.

James grinned and switched the subject back to tennis. 'You lost it in the vital seventh game of the second set!' he reminded her. 'You served those two double faults.'

She nodded. 'I know, I know; I lost concentration.'

The sound of footsteps on the drive interrupted them. Through the window they could see John Hardy come bounding up to the door. They dashed out, glad to see him looking flushed and excited for once.

'What's got into you?' James demanded. He dragged John inside. 'Did you finish your project?'

John sank breathlessly into a chair. He ran a hand through his wavy hair. 'No, it's not that. I've just got back from town, and guess what?'

'What?' Mandy pushed a drink of juice across the table in his direction.

'There's a new pet shop that's just opened up on the High Street!'

'We know. Pets' Parlour,' James cut in.

'That's the one. But guess what, guess what!' John was almost spluttering with excitement. He unzipped his jacket and rested on the two back legs of his chair. 'They've got rabbits! Rabbits in the window! Little brown ones! For sale!

They're selling pet rabbits!'

'That's Button and Barney,' Mandy grinned. 'Anyway, that's what we call them.' She glanced across at James.

'You mean you've already seen them?' He looked astonished that his news wasn't new.

She nodded. 'Last week. I suppose that means that no one's come along and bought them yet.'

'Yes, thank heavens!' John gasped.

'Why, what are you up to now? Don't you want them to go to a good home then?' She glanced across again at James. What was going on in John's mind?

'No, I want them to come to *my* home!' he declared. He laughed out loud at their surprise.

'*You* want them?' she repeated.

'Yes, why not? I know lots of stuff about rabbits now. I can look after them. I went straight in and paid the money and asked the woman in the shop to keep them to one side for me!' John's face had come alive. He leapt up from his chair. 'Come on, you two! Let's go home and tell Dad!'

'But . . . !' Mandy felt a niggling doubt rise to the surface. What would happen to Button and Barney when John was away at school?

'Come on, what are you waiting for? Come and help me explain to my dad!'

Mandy shrugged, James nodded. 'You seem to have made up your own mind already!' he said.

'You bet!' John ran ahead. 'I bought them with my own money! Button and Barney are going to be all mine! I'll build a hutch, they can live in the garden! This is going to be great!'

Mandy and James followed him up the lane. She kept her fingers crossed for John as they headed for the Fox and Goose, but she had a nasty feeling that it wouldn't be quite that simple. Keeping pets when you had to go away to school was complicated. How would John feel when he had to leave them behind and set off for the Lake District? And who would be left to take good care of Button and Barney?

Five

'Don't be daft, John!' Julian Hardy stood in the kitchen at the back of the pub, armed with two massive plates of ham sandwiches. 'How can we keep pet rabbits here? Where on earth would we put them, for a start?' He was on his way back into the bar to cope with the busy lunch-time rush.

'In the garden, in a hutch.' John's eager face began to shut down. He glanced at Mandy and James, who hung back outside. 'They wouldn't be any trouble, honest!'

'And what happens when you're away at school? Who would you get to feed them then?' Mr Hardy pushed open the inner door with his foot. He balanced the plates carefully. '*And* keep them clean? *And* make sure they got some exercise?' He waited a second for John to see sense.

Mandy sighed. She'd feared this was going to happen.

'But, Dad, it doesn't take long. They're dead easy to look after. Aren't they, Mandy?'

She nodded, but she could see they were fighting a losing battle. Button and Barney would have to spend more time in the pet shop until another kindly owner came along.

'See – Mandy knows! And I've already paid for them, Dad. I can't back out now!'

Mandy looked at James. She could tell that his heart had sunk as low as hers. John was in for another big disappointment.

'Look, can we talk about this some other time?' Mr Hardy was beginning to frown. He hopped and wobbled on one foot, struggling to keep his balance. Then Sara opened the door from the far side. She stopped short, immediately sensing that something was wrong.

'I need to know straight away!' John persisted. 'Rabbits are my main project for science this year. I'll be at home for the whole of the summer to look after them. And I can come back for more weekends and half-terms. You'll hardly have to do anything!'

'That's what you say now, and it's all very well. But just you wait; it'd be me looking after them most of the time. I'd bet a lot of money on it!'

'Honestly, Dad! Listen, they're fantastic, aren't they, Mandy? They're brown all over and really friendly. They need a good home; they're getting bored cooped up in the pet shop all day long. I want to look after them!'

Mr Hardy sighed. 'Listen, once and for all, John. I said no! It's not practical. So you'll just have to go straight back to the shop, tell them you changed your mind, and get your money back!' He marched on through the door. It was his final word.

Sara hovered nervously, just inside the kitchen door. She peered into John's face. 'Never mind. Let me have a talk to him for you; see what I can do.'

Mandy noticed that John, who was quite small himself, easily reached Sara's shoulder. She was a shy, bright, bird-like woman.

'If you leave it a day or two, perhaps I can talk him round,' she suggested.

John hung his head. He was silent.

Oh no! Mandy thought. She half expected to see John rush off again.

But he kept his head low and stood there thinking. 'It wouldn't do any good,' he said at last.

'How do you know? You could let me have a go at least.' Sara spoke gently, pushing her loose hair back behind her ears.

'What for?' he demanded. He looked her straight in the eye. 'Do you like rabbits, or something?'

Sara's face broke into a smile. 'As a matter of fact, yes! I had some myself when I was a kid!'

'Hmm,' John scuffed at the table leg. He hung his head again, then sighed. 'No thanks, don't bother.'

Mandy frowned. She wanted to shake some common sense into him, but she knew how upset he must be.

'Why not? Since I'm going to be living here after the wedding, I could easily take care of a couple of little rabbits when you're away. No problem!'

'They won't always be little!' John broke in scornfully. 'They'll grow. And anyway, I said no thanks!'

'OK.' Sara backed off, ready to retreat into the bar.

'Anyway, you'd never be able to persuade him. You don't know my dad like I do. Once he's made up his mind, he never changes it!' He gave her a haughty look, back to his old buttoned-up self. 'Come on, James, you haven't seen the latest photographs. Have you got five minutes to come up and have a look?' He went off, quietly accepting his father's decision.

Mandy shot a wide-eyed look in Sara's direction. 'Time for a juice?' Sara asked.

Mandy nodded. John was hard to work out. What had happened to his bubbly excitement over Button and Barney? He seemed just to have swallowed it as he led James up the narrow stairs.

'I'm not getting any better at it, am I?' Sara sighed and stared out through the back door. Tiny pink and white blossom flowers framed their view of the old-fashioned walled garden. 'Julian and I get married in June, during John's half-term holiday, but I'm beginning to think he'll even refuse to show up for the wedding!'

'I just think it takes a long time to get to know him,' Mandy admitted.

'If ever!' Sara sighed again and shrugged.

'What happened to his real mum?' Mandy asked. As far back as she could remember, there had always been just John and his dad at the Fox and Goose.

'It was very sad. She was badly injured in a motorway crash. She was unconscious in hospital for five months, then she died.'

Mandy greeted the news in silence.

Sara continued in a slow, quiet voice. 'From what your mum has told me about it, Julian and John got quite a lot of money from the insurance firm after the crash. It helps to pay John's school fees and so on. But of course it never made up for losing his mum.'

Mandy nodded. She felt tears come to her eyes, hot and shining. '*My* real mum and dad were killed in a car crash,' she said at last. 'I'm adopted. I was only a baby when it happened, so I don't remember.'

'So was John. In fact the crash happened before he was born. He was lucky to survive.'

Mandy nodded. Now she understood much more about John's moods; his long silences, his serious gaze. 'Does he like his school?' she asked, trying to find something good to say about the whole sad situation.

But Sara shook her head. 'Not much. It's because Julian has to work all hours in the pub;

he feels John gets a better deal away at Grange.
And between you and me, I think poor John feels
a bit guilty about not liking school as much as he
should. After all, it was his mother's death that
paid for it.'

Mandy nodded and sighed. 'Yes, poor John.'

She felt Sara give her a quick hug and saw her
brush a forefinger across her own lashes.

'Never mind, perhaps things will work out in
the end,' Sara said quietly as James and John came
back downstairs.

John gave her a cool stare and walked on out of
the house. 'I'm on my way up to High Cross. Does
anyone feel like coming along?' he said to James
and Mandy in his distant, couldn't-care-less way.

Next day, it was James's idea to head back to the
Fox and Goose after they'd helped Mr Hope on
his afternoon round. 'Let's see how John's getting
on,' he suggested.

Mandy readily agreed.

They found Mr Hardy busy shifting crates and
stacking them by the side door, ready for
collection. John was up at High Cross again, he
told them. 'I don't know what's got into him lately.'
He shook his head, and stared into the distance.

Mandy glanced at James. 'Did he go back to
the pet shop to tell them he can't have Button
and Barney after all?' she asked.

Mr Hardy shook his head. 'I've been thinking
about that, though. Maybe I was a bit harsh,' he
confessed.

'Here, here!' Sara popped her head round the
door, a smile on her face. She grinned at Mandy
and James. 'Hello, you two! That's just what I
was thinking!' she told her fiancé. She put a
cardboard box full of crisps on a nearby table
and came out to join them. 'You could still
change your mind, Julian. Give John a chance

to look after those rabbits. It'll do him good.'

'Hmm.' Mr Hardy frowned.

Mandy showed James her fingers crossed behind her back. John's dad seemed to be weakening.

Sara went confidently on. 'He's proved it's not just a whim,' she reminded Julian Hardy. 'Rabbits mean an awful lot to John. He really cares. OK, so he shouldn't have gone ahead and paid for Button and Barney without asking you first. I agree about that. But he was obviously carried away. Poor kid. I can't get his face out of my mind when you told him he couldn't bring them home!' She paused.

Me neither! Mandy thought. There was the hurt look, then the blank expression came down like a shutter. 'Poor John,' she said under her breath.

'OK, OK!' Mr Hardy put up his hands to defend himself. He sighed. 'I was only thinking how hard things had been up till now. I mean, having pets really was out of the question before I met you, Sara. I didn't have time for anything except work!'

Sara went up and put an arm round his waist.

'But now?' James prompted. He stood alongside Mandy with his own fingers crossed.

Mr Hardy's face broke into a smile. 'Now it's

different! Now we can all muck in together. And rabbits are pretty straightforward to look after, aren't they?' He turned to Mandy.

'Nothing to it!' she vowed. 'You just have to keep them clean, warm and well fed!'

'OK, that does it!' He gave Sara a hug. 'I've changed my mind. Button and Barney can come!'

James leapt in the air like a footballer who'd scored a winning goal. Mandy shot straight off across the car park.

'Hang on, where are you going?' James yelled.

'To tell John, of course! I can, can't I?' She checked with his dad.

Everyone grinned. 'Yes, go on! Run up to High Cross and tell him the good news!' Mr Hardy agreed. 'And tell him to get himself back down here. It looks like it's going to rain before too long!'

They ran straight through the village, and up the hill to the remote farm. Then they headed quickly for the far pasture, to John's favourite look-out spot.

There, by the wide bole of an old ash tree, they found his purple and green rucksack propped on top of his green jacket. But there was no sign of John himself.

'He must have gone across to the nursery

warren,' Mandy said. She peeked inside the bag, surprised to see that he'd left his expensive camera unguarded. He was getting careless. She knew that he was determined to study and record each stage of the baby rabbits' progress, but he ought to have taken more care about his belongings.

Mandy and James strode along the wall side, careful to steer clear of the area where the yearlings had set up a new warren. Mandy was bursting to give John the good news about Button and Barney. 'Where's he got to?' she whispered, as they made their way across to the nursery.

They wove their way through five or six low hawthorn trees at the far end of Lydia's pasture. Beyond that, there was a low, rocky ridge running up to the moor top at right angles to it. It made a white ledge that dipped down into rough, unfarmed land. Few people strayed beyond this point, just the odd walker and one or two sheep farmers with their dogs, so the rabbits used it as a safe, quiet place to rear their young. Mandy stood on the ridge and put her hand to her eyes to scan the horizon. She was downwind of the warren, and knew that she was too far away to disturb the rabbits at their evening feed.

Where are you, John? Mandy was starting to feel impatient with him for not being in any of the usual places. Heavy, cold drops of rain began to fall. They made dark blotches on the white rock. She zipped up her jacket against the wind. In the distance she could see a dozen or so adult does hopping uneasily out of their burrows; ears up, back legs kicking. She knew they didn't like the rain, but she guessed there was something extra in the air which made them nervous. None of the babies had followed their mothers into the open. Mandy and James squatted to watch them.

Soon they spotted a few rabbits busily scratching openings in a patch of loose, bare earth, close to a hawthorn tree. They were making new burrows for their litters. But they too kept stopping, sitting up and glancing round, ready to bolt.

'What is it? What's happening?' James whispered. They listened hard for any unusual sound.

Maybe John was hiding upwind of the rabbits by mistake. 'Perhaps they can smell him,' Mandy suggested.

An explosion ripped through the air. High and sharp, it rattled down the hillside from the ridge above. Mandy felt her stomach lurch as she recognised the sound of farmers' guns. The rabbits scattered in an instant. They were gone. The hillside stood eerily empty.

A figure started up from behind a rock. It was John. He began to run up the hill. More gunshots echoed down the valley side.

'John!' Mandy stood and yelled as loud as she could. She and James set off after him.

Another shot cracked through the dull air above. 'John, wait!' she yelled. The wind caught her voice and whipped it back down the hillside into the valley bottom.

He ran, fast as a hare, over the rough ground. The rain had brought down a mist which clung to the ridge and hid the men with the shotguns. Soon John too was a pale figure vanishing into the mist.

'Come back, you'll get shot!' The stuttering guns rattled on. The men were out to get rabbits, to thin down their numbers. Farmers hated rabbits on their land; they ate crops and ruined the soil.

Mandy and James ran and stumbled up the hill. Their breath became short, their legs weakened. They just managed to keep John in view as he leapt over rocks, across rough grass; head back, feet pounding over the distance between him and the sound of guns. He was yelling at them to stop.

Another gust of wind swirled the mist clear of the ground. A dog barked and growled. Mandy saw the black outlines of three men with shotguns to their shoulders, standing on the ridge. Their barrels were tilted down towards the nursery warren. John hurtled straight at them.

Mandy jumped down a drop of about a metre, from a boulder on to a soft bed of couch grass. She stumbled forward, then pushed herself on after John. Nothing would stop him. He seemed to have lost his senses, still running, and only seconds away from the men on the ridge.

'Hold it, there's a kid down there!' the nearest man warned. They let their guns drop to waist height. But they stood, feet planted wide apart, glaring at John. One kept a squat white bulldog close to heel. It growled and bared its teeth as John kept on coming.

'You want to get yourself killed?' the first man yelled in a rough voice. 'Because you're going the right way about it down there!'

John ran at him. 'Don't shoot the rabbits!' He was beside himself with fright.

The man braced himself. He slung his gun over

his shoulder. 'Now, steady on!' he shouted. 'Just hold it where you are. We've got a job to do here, and we aim to do it. So just stand out of our way, sonny, and let us get on with it!'

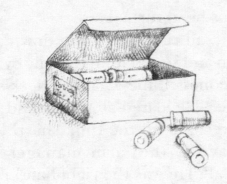

Six

Mandy didn't stop to think. Her long legs carried her swiftly over the last stretch of rough ground. John had got himself into deep trouble with the men with the guns. She went straight at him from behind, flung herself forward and threw her arms round his waist. She tackled him to the ground.

The first man strode down the hill towards them. The bulldog growled and snapped. James caught up with Mandy and began to pull her and John to their feet. Mandy could feel her heart thumping, her knees hurting from the heavy fall. Still she clung on to John, in case he struggled up and kept on charging. But he stood there gasping, his head turned away.

'All right, all right, just calm down!' The man came down and seized John roughly by the elbow. 'Will someone tell me what the heck's going on round here?' He glared at Mandy and James.

Mandy recognised the thin, sharp features of Dennis Saville, the farm manager at Upper Welford Hall. He was the right-hand man of the owner, Sam Western. She knew him as a hard-hearted, no-nonsense sort who simply carried out his boss's orders. No doubt Mr Western had sent Dennis and a couple of lads up on to the ridge with orders to thin down the local rabbit population.

'It's OK, let me talk to John,' she said. She stooped to brush herself down. She and John were covered in dirt. His face was marked and scratched, and he still struggled as Dennis tried to restrain him.

Another figure, one of the two stocky lads in jeans and heavy boots, came lumbering down the hill. He held his gun under his arm and kicked loose stones as he pulled himself up short alongside Mandy's little group. 'What's up?' he demanded. 'Has the kid gone nuts or something?'

'No!' James was stung into a reply. 'Just leave

him alone, will you? He was only doing what he could to save the rabbits!'

'What?' the lad jeered, as if unable to believe his ears. 'Save rabbits? You must be joking!'

'It's their nursery warren down there, full of babies!' Mandy reminded him.

'So?' The lad stood with one hand in the pocket of his denim jacket, letting the shiny steel barrel of his shotgun drop forward. The polished wooden butt rested under his arm.

'They're just a few weeks old. They're still helpless!'

'So?' He stood and sneered. 'All the better for us!'

John shoved his shoulder against Dennis Saville's chest to try and push him off. His face was drained and white, with a bright red graze on one cheek where he'd fallen against a rough stone.

'Steady on!' Dennis insisted. He was wiry and strong, and kept a firm hold of John's arm. John beat at his tight grasp with his spare hand. 'Now if you don't calm down, I'll set the dog on you!' the manager threatened. Above them, the second lad held the bulldog by its steel-studded collar. It crouched low, ready to leap forward.

'John!' Mandy pleaded. She caught hold of his sleeve. 'Wait a minute, let's just try to explain!' She waited for him to stop pushing, and watched, as slowly the older man released him.

John's breath came out in harsh gasps. His chest and shoulders heaved, but he looked stunned now, rather than wild with fear. His hands shook as he tried to brush mud from his sweater.

'Mr Saville, John's doing a study on the rabbits for a school project. He's been hard at work up here for more than a week now.' She tried to sound calm and reasonable.

The man allowed his frown to relax a fraction. 'Has he now? Yes, that'd be right. I've seen him coming by the big house with his camera often enough. Does Miss Fawcett know you're here? You'd need her permission to cross that last field.'

'Yes, she knows.' Mandy could see that John was still too shocked to answer.

The lad laughed out loud. 'Not much use expecting her to take a gun to a few rabbits,' he scoffed. '*She* probably feeds 'em dandelions and invites 'em in the house. She's as daft as a brush, just like him!' He pointed with the gun at John. 'They're both off their heads, if you ask me!'

'Dean, that'll do!' Dennis Saville warned. 'What

Lydia Fawcett gets up to on her own land is her business, and we can't do a thing about it if she chooses not to shoot rabbits. But this is common land, and up here we've every right to try and cut down on this year's young 'uns.'

'But why?' Mandy pleaded. 'What harm are they doing to you if they dig their warren way up here?'

Dennis Saville gave an exasperated sigh. 'They don't stay put here on this stretch, do they now? Soon as they've found their feet these young ones come scampering down to the Hall, looking for whatever they can find. Nice juicy fruit from the currant bushes, anything they can sink their teeth into, little devils. And they dig up the lawn and make a right mess of things. Can you blame Mr Western for wanting to get rid of them?'

Mandy wasn't convinced. She thought a rabbit had as much right to be where he or she wanted as any local landowner. But she bit her tongue. 'Can't you put wire netting round the fruit bushes?' she asked, looking for a logical way out.

Dean snorted and stamped off back up the hill. 'Why are we wasting time with these loonies?' he asked in a loud voice. He released the barrel on his gun, ready to load more shot.

John seemed to come back to life at the sound

of the click of metal. He turned on Dennis Saville.
'You're not going to let them start up again, are
you?'

The farm manager shrugged. 'Listen, why don't
you three just move off back to High Cross for
half an hour? There'll be plenty of rabbits left for
you to carry on studying, even after we've finished
here.'

Mandy felt her blood run cold. She turned to
James. 'Tell them that's not the point!' The mist
was lifting and the clouds rolling away. Soon the
rabbits would get back their nerve and emerge
from the nursery warren.

'It's no use, they won't listen!' James turned and walked three or four paces downhill. 'But it's just like you said,' he told the farm manager. 'This is common ground. We've got as much right to be here as you lot. And we're not shifting! This is where we're staying, right here!' He stood and glared back up the hill. Behind and below him, the land kept its eerie silence.

'Good idea!' Mandy followed his lead. 'Come on, John! If they won't listen to reason, we'll have to find another way of stopping them!' She joined James, leaping on to a low boulder, and looking determined to see off the three men with their guns.

Saville stared down at them and shook his head. He put his hands in his pockets and strode back up to the ridge. 'Down! Stay down!' he ordered the dog. For a few moments he stood and talked with the two lads.

'I only hope this works!' Mandy whispered to John and James.

'Well, *I'm* not moving,' John replied between clenched teeth. He stood alongside James and Mandy. 'James is right; we're staying right where we are!'

'Forever?' Mandy bit her bottom lip. What had

they got themselves into now? The men were still discussing their next tactic.

'For as long as *they* stay!' John promised. 'And I'll be here for as long as there's any chance of them coming back!'

'Could be a long wait.' Mandy glanced at him. The wind had brought colour back to his cheeks. His head was up, his face looked brave and clear. 'Anyway, good for you. After tonight we can get Lydia to use her new phone to send down warnings to Animal Ark or to the Fox and Goose, whenever she sees them crossing the back of her place with their guns. It'll mostly be in the evenings. And we'll drop what we're doing and be up here like a shot – oops!' She laughed at her choice of words.

'Great!' The wind blew John's hair straight back. 'As long as we're around they won't be able to shoot any more rabbits!'

'Maybe!' James added, in his sensible, clear way.

They waited, confidence rising, and they watched as Dennis Saville shrugged and muttered one last instruction to the lads. Then he led them and the dog off over the ridge out of sight.

Mandy, James and John cheered. 'Brilliant!' John cried. 'That's the first battle won, at any rate!'

With huge sighs of relief, they ran back to the ash trees and John's usual lookout spot. They crouched down. Soon peace and quiet returned to the high fields. No more gunshots. No more man-smell to scare the rabbits. Now the pasture and the hills beyond were alive with mother and baby rabbits, lolloping, crouching, scuffling, nibbling, nipping, and combing their ears in the calm evening air.

'One more thing!' Mandy said, when she could catch her breath at last. James studied the rabbits with a small, secret grin on his face as he listened to her. 'Ask us why we came up here when we did! Go on, ask us!' She couldn't hide her own excitement at the news she was about to give.

John dragged his own glance away from the rabbits. 'Go on, then. Why?'

'Your dad sent us.'

'Oh!' he grunted.

'To tell you—'

'To get back home for supper?' he growled.

'No! To tell you you can keep Button and Barney after all!'

'Where? At home?' John's mouth hung open. He grabbed hold of Mandy's arm.

'Yes, at home! He changed his mind!'

John whooped and fell flat on his back. 'Tell me I'm not dreaming!' he gasped.

'You're not dreaming. You can keep the rabbits,' James repeated. 'Come on, let's go!'

They gathered John's things, dragged him up off the ground, and headed for home.

But Lydia cut them off as they made their way down past High Cross. 'You three haven't been getting yourselves shot at, have you?' she called. 'I heard all the noise up there!' She came up to them with a worried frown.

'No!' Mandy laughed. 'Not quite.' She told Lydia what had happened.

'Hmm.' Lydia was still frowning. 'I'm on your side,' she told them. 'Call me soft-hearted, but I hate the idea of taking a gun to the poor creatures as much as you three do. On the other hand, I don't want you to risk getting yourselves shot!'

'We won't!' James promised. 'But if you do see Dennis Saville up there again, can you ring and tell us? We've got a plan to stop them shooting in the nursery warren.'

Lydia nodded. She took John inside to bathe his grazed face in warm water and disinfectant.

'We just need to be there. That would be enough,' Mandy explained. 'They'd never carry on shooting while we're there.'

'Let me think about it,' Lydia said. 'Perhaps I can come up with a better plan.'

'What?' John winced as she dabbed his graze with cotton-wool.

'Maybe I can get them to give into the temptation of freshly-baked scones whenever they're passing this way. That would soon put paid to their rabbiting; hot tea and fresh scones!' Lydia's eyes twinkled.

'I'm not sure.' John stood up and looked at Mandy and James.

'Well, leave it with me. Perhaps I can think of something else as well.' Lydia drained off the bowl of water at the sink.

Mandy nodded. She could trust her old friend to help them out. 'Come on,' she said, anxious to get John back home.

They said goodbye to Lydia and ran on, down past Upper Welford Hall, then past Beacon House. Mandy waved to Imogen Parker Smythe. The little girl swung moodily to and fro on the swing her father had slung from a branch of one of their huge beech trees. The plump, pig-tailed seven-year-old was slow to wave back. She had her heated swimming-pool and her enormous garden, but she didn't seem to have any friends who would come and play. Mandy usually saw her all alone, scowling, or running inside to her mum, whenever she passed.

Mandy, James and John gathered speed down the steep hill, and ran down past the golf-club, past the tennis-courts, and over the old bridge to the crossroads and the Fox and Goose.

Julian Hardy looked relaxed and comfortable in a blue open-necked shirt as he lounged in front of the television. In the bar, his staff were getting ready for the evening trade. Sara sat at a table by the window. She was writing out wedding invitations on squares of cream-coloured card edged with silver. She looked up and smiled at the three of them, then laid down her pen.

'Hello, son!' Mr Hardy made room for John on the sofa. He put an arm along the back of it, close to his shoulder. 'Hey, have you been in the wars?' he asked. He'd noticed the raw graze on John's cheek.

'I slipped on a rock, that's all,' John said. 'Something had scared the rabbits, and I was just trying to sort it out when I slipped and lost my footing.' He stared meaningfully at Mandy and James, as if to warn them not to go into detail.

'Well, never mind, no real harm done.' Mr Hardy grinned across at Sara. 'When shall we go and collect Barney and Button, then?'

'First thing tomorrow?' she suggested. Mandy could see that Sara was going to enjoy this almost as much as anyone else in the room.

John's grin stretched from ear to ear. 'Fantastic! Thanks, Dad!'

'Thank Mandy and James, and Sara here. She threatened to divorce me if I said no to the rabbits!'

'And we're not even married yet!' she joked.

John turned towards her. 'Thanks, Sara.' He looked round the room at them all. 'Oh, great! Oh, fantastic! Oh, brilliant! . . . Wow!' he said.

Seven

'Nice to see that you two have made friends again,' Jean commented. She peered over her glasses from behind the reception desk at Animal Ark.

James Hunter had arrived early for the trip into Walton. Sara had promised to wait at the Fox and Goose while Mandy and James travelled over to the pet shop with John and his father. She knew they could help choose the right food and so on, so they'd arranged to meet up at the pub at nine o'clock.

Now James coloured up under Jean's gaze.

'We never fell out in the first place!' Mandy objected. 'James has always been my best friend!'

'I've just remembered something! I've got to padlock my bike!' James darted outside.

Mandy flicked her hair back from her forehead. 'See what you've done? You've embarrassed him!'

Jean smiled. 'He's such a nice boy, James Hunter. I was quite lost without him last week, when he went away and you seemed to have taken up with the Hardy boy. I missed his smiling face!' She smiled. Her own grandchildren lived too far away for her to see them often.

'John Hardy is nice too,' Mandy protested. 'Once you get to know him.' She remembered to write a name and phone number into the appointment book from a phone call she'd taken just before James arrived. 'You know, he was great yesterday. He stopped Mr Western's men from shooting all the rabbits up at High Cross!' She delivered the tale of John's heroic dash up the hill. ' . . . And then he came face to face with the barrel of a gun and he never even flinched! Imagine! Only inches away from his nose. It was just like on TV!'

Jean tutted. 'You're exaggerating again, dear.'

'No, I'm not. Oh, well, maybe just a teeny bit! But most of it's true! And now he's going to get the reward he deserves. His dad says he can have the two baby rabbits from the pet shop in town. Isn't that great?'

Jean's eyebrows shot up. 'I thought Julian Hardy had enough on his plate, poor man, coping with everything single-handed.' Jean went to straighten the chairs back against the wall, ready for surgery to begin.

'Well, he won't be single-handed after he marries Sara, will he? And *she* likes pets. And anyway, he did say yes. We were there at the time!' Mandy checked her watch and ran a brush through her hair, getting ready to go.

'Hmm, well, he must be going soft in his old age, then.' Jean chatted on regardless. 'Funny that; rabbits seem to be popular at the moment. I had a phone call only yesterday from someone who wanted to know about inoculations for them, and so on. The little girl was so excited she could hardly get the word out. I told her to bring her rabbits along to the surgery this Saturday.'

'Well, I'm not surprised they're so popular. They're gorgeous creatures.' Mandy thought of the fluffy brown babies in Pets' Parlour, and of her own three rabbits happily munching oats out in the back garden. She glanced out of the window on to the drive. 'Here's Simon now!' She went out to join James, and they crossed paths with Animal Ark's young nurse who, as ever, looked bright and cheerful as he turned up for work.

'Don't do anything I wouldn't do!' he called after them.

'As if!' Mandy replied. They were in high spirits themselves as they headed for the Fox and Goose.

They rode over to Walton in Mr Hardy's smart green car. John sat in the front, silent with excitement, almost gripping the sides of his seat in his eagerness to be there. No one said much during the fifteen minute journey; they just looked out across the moor, spotting curlews overhead, plus the odd seagull, and high above, a sparrow-hawk gliding on the air currents.

Mr Hardy parked in the town's central carpark. Together they crossed the main street. Mandy waved at Mr Cecil, hard at work inside his chocolate shop. He was filling the windows with home-made chocolate assortment boxes. Down the road they could spot the red lettering over the window of Pets' Parlour, and the much dimmer, more cluttered interior.

'Come on!' John insisted, breaking into a run for the last few metres.

They looked into the window at the muddle of dog leads, baskets, mice cages and budgerigar mirrors. There was a gap where Button and Barney should have been. John shot an anxious look at his father.

'They must still be inside,' Mr Hardy remarked. 'Having breakfast. Come on, let's go in and see.' He opened the door to the stuffy smell of birdseed and fish food. Across the dark room, the blue, red and silver fishes darted across their bubbling tank. James was the last one in. He closed the door to the loud tinkle of the shop bell.

'Yes, please? Can I help you?' Geoff, the friendly young shopkeeper, came out from the back room, his red shirt covered in stray wisps of straw, his sleeves rolled back. 'I hope I didn't keep you waiting.'

Julian Hardy nudged John forward to the counter. Mandy and James stayed quietly in the background. Their eyes swept the shelves for any sign of the rabbit hutch. A nervous feeling had begun to clutch hold of Mandy's stomach.

'I've come about the rabbits,' John began. He put both hands on the counter to steady his nerves.

Geoff studied him more closely. 'I'm sorry,

which rabbits?' He looked puzzled.

John carried on. 'I know it must have seemed a bit strange, me not coming straight back for them yesterday, but can I collect them now, please? I'd like to take them home.'

Mr Hardy stepped forward to help out. 'Actually, to be fair, it was me who caused the delay, not John. I thought we wouldn't be able to cope with Button and Barney. But then I thought better of it. He can have them after all, and we promise five-star accommodation at the Fox and Goose!' He jollied the mood, which seemed to have gone awkward and flat.

Behind the counter, Geoff began to frown. 'Button and Barney? The little brown rabbits?' He coughed and cleared the back of his throat, then shook his head.

Mandy's chest thudded; one dreadful, heart stopping moment.

Geoff went on. 'Look, I'm sorry, but you're too late. I'm afraid I've already sold those two, just yesterday afternoon. Don't worry, it was to a very good owner.' He shrugged and looked uncomfortable. 'You're out of luck there, I'm afraid.'

The life drained from John's face. His eyes

stared slowly round the shelves, as if this was some terrible joke and Button and Barney could be found lurking in a dark corner. 'But I already paid for them!' he stammered. 'They were *my* rabbits! You can't have sold them to someone else!'

Mandy saw from the stricken look on her friend's face that his world had collapsed. He stared as Geoff explained what must have happened. 'It wasn't me you bought them from, was it?'

Slowly John shook his head. 'No, it was someone else. A lady.'

Geoff nodded. 'That was Mrs Kearney. She was looking after things in the shop that day. She obviously forgot to tell me that she'd sold the rabbits to you!' He sighed and then shrugged at Julian Hardy. 'I'm very sorry. He's obviously upset, and I don't blame him. It's a bad mistake on our part. But I'll tell you what!' He turned to John. 'I'll put your name to the top of the list, and I'll tell you when the next two rabbits come up for sale. I'm expecting to take in another litter in a couple of weeks,' he said. 'You could come back then. In the meantime, I'll refund your money.'

'I'll be away at school,' John said in a hollow voice.

'But I can bring Mandy and James back here,' his father offered. 'They can help me choose some more rabbits.' He stood, hands in pockets. 'Look, John, it's not a disaster. We can still get you some pets.'

He shook his head. 'No thanks.'

'Why not?'

'Because it's Button and Barney I want. I bought them myself, and I don't feel the same about having any others. Thanks.' He turned stiffly away.

Julian Hardy shrugged at the shopkeeper. 'It looks as though we'll have to leave it for now,' he said.

Geoff nodded. 'Sorry about the mix-up.' He spread his palms and returned the shrug. 'I do feel really bad about it.'

'Never mind, it can't be helped. It doesn't matter.' He smiled and herded James, Mandy and John out of the shop.

Mandy heard the doorbell ring behind them. *Yes, it does matter!* she thought. *It means the whole world to John!*

She glanced at James, uncertain what to do next. Button and Barney had been whisked away from under their noses. She felt empty and sad, and yet she could only guess how disappointed John himself must feel. They trailed back to the car park in complete silence.

'Sorry,' Mr Hardy sighed, as they sank into their car seats. 'I can see that this is all my fault. I shouldn't have held things up. I really am sorry, John!'

John pulled his seat-belt across his chest. 'Oh no, not at all,' he said. 'It's nobody's fault. It's just one of those things.'

How can he say that? Mandy wondered. She knew John must be feeling dreadful!

When they got back to the Fox and Goose, John got out of the car and went straight to his room. Mandy looked at Mr Hardy, who nodded that she should follow him up. She took the stairs two at a time.

Mandy opened John's bedroom door. He sat cross-legged on the floor. The walls were covered in diagrams and sketches. Rabbits stared down at him from the bathroom door, from his wonderful photographs still scattered all over the carpet. He was surrounded by them. But he hadn't got what he really wanted. All he wanted was Button and Barney to clean and feed and care for. Two live creatures to help him get over the changes that had come charging into his life.

'I thought you might like some company,' said Mandy.

'Thanks, Mandy, but I'd rather be on my own,' John replied in a quiet voice.

'I understand,' Mandy said. 'Call me tomorrow, and we can go up to High Cross together.' John nodded a reply, but Mandy wondered if he really would call. She quietly closed his bedroom door.

Feeling rather helpless, Mandy went downstairs.

After the disaster at the pet shop, Mandy and James didn't hear a word from John. Sara popped into Animal Ark for coffee one morning and told Mandy's mum that he was drifting round the house like a ghost. 'Like he's not really there,' she said. 'And he's out all the time; every chance he gets, he's up roaming round on that farm. His dad's nearly out of his mind with worry. We really don't know what to do.'

Emily Hope gave Sara a sympathetic smile. 'Give him time,' she advised. 'There are so many new things for him to get used to all at once.'

Mrs Hope saw her old school-friend to the door, and shook her head sadly. As she went to begin surgery, Mandy realised that even her mum had no decent solutions.

She heard too from Lydia that John Hardy now spent all his time among the High Cross warrens. Lydia rang up one teatime, worried that she hadn't seen Mandy up there with him during the last few days. 'I thought you might be ill,' she said. 'I got so used to you coming along too that I began to wonder what had happened. Have you two fallen out?'

'No. But John said he wanted to be by himself. He said he can concentrate on his work better that way.' Mandy fiddled with the half eaten cheese-on-toast on her plate. She'd lost her appetite and spent her own time worrying what was happening to John. Lydia's phone call did nothing to put her mind at rest.

'Hmm. It's not good for a boy of his age to be alone so much.' Lydia let a big pause develop before she went on. 'Mandy, I don't suppose you could—'

She jumped in without allowing Lydia to finish. 'Come up to High Cross? Yes, of course I can. James is here too. We'll both be right up!' She jumped to her feet and looked in James's direction.

'Oh, good. I'm sure it'll help to cheer him up. He looks so . . . lonely, you know. It's very cut off up here. I'm sure he'd prefer to have some company.'

'OK?' Mandy signalled to James. He nodded. 'OK, Lydia, we're on our way.' She put down the phone. Whether or not John would prefer to have company, Mandy leapt at Lydia's suggestion.

She and James hopped on to their bikes and pedalled up the hill. It was evening; John was certain to be hanging round the warrens at this time of day. The rabbits would be feeding and basking in the low sun. That, anyway, would be a sight worth seeing.

Sure enough, John's rucksack sat abandoned at the foot of the ash tree. Down past the farm, they could see Lydia leading the goats in for milking. Then, higher up, beyond the far pasture, they spotted John. He sat still as a statue on a low rock, huddled over a sketchbook. All round him rabbits grazed, nipping and nibbling at the grass. The hillside would spring to life whenever they moved; hopping, kicking and darting to the next juicy leaf. John was there right in their midst, but they ignored him.

'He looks like part of the scenery,' James

whispered. 'I bet he wishes he could stay here forever.'

'Poor John,' Mandy sighed. 'Let's wait here until he moves. We don't want to scare them all away.' They stood by a wall, watching and waiting.

When the rabbits sat bolt upright, twitching their ears to listen out for danger, Mandy and James saw John glance behind. There must have been a tiny sound, up over the horizon. The rabbits stared and twitched. Another sound. They fled. Dozens of white tails bobbed and were gone. John stood up and turned to face the high ridge.

Two figures appeared. They carried shotguns and swaggered down the hill.

'Dean and his friend!' Mandy gasped. She ran forward across the empty pasture. 'Not again!' But this time there was no farm manager to keep the lads in check.

'I think that's Steve Burnley with him,' James told her.

The two youths were bearing down on John, who just stood waiting, camera round his neck, sketchbook at his side.

'He got expelled for bullying in his last year. I know his younger brother, Frankie.' James sounded worried. 'Have you seen their guns?'

'Yes, and I've got this feeling that John's likely to do something rash again, the strange mood he's been in lately!' Mandy began to shout and wave her arms, trying to distract Dean and Steve's attention.

But John turned on them as they clambered over the last low wall on to the common ground. 'Go away!' he yelled. 'I can deal with this!'

On a level with John, Dean came to a halt. 'Not you again!' he said scornfully. 'I've had just about enough of you!'

'Tough!' John retorted. 'Because I'm not moving!'

Dean laughed. 'Big man!'

John stood his ground.

Dean's friend, Steve, curled his lip and took up position on the far side of John.

'Wait!' James warned Mandy. 'Better see what happens next!' He pulled her to a halt.

'I said I'm not moving!' John insisted. His chin was up, he stared back at them.

'Do you think we can't make you!' Dean taunted. He tapped the barrel of his gun, then grinned.

James and Mandy gasped.

'Look, sonny, just stand out of the way, why don't you?' Steve advised. 'We've got a job to do here; Mr Western's orders. And we always do what we're told, don't we, Dean?' Swiftly he swung his gun round in the direction of some distant hawthorns. He took a shot at them. The sound cracked and echoed across the valley.

Mandy jumped, but John didn't move a muscle. She half turned away, afraid to look.

'Go on, shoot! But I'm still not moving!' he yelled. 'I'm staying right where I am!'

'Now, no one's shooting anything round here!' A calm voice started up close by, just behind James. Lydia had marched up from the bottom pasture, leading Houdini on a short rope. The goat's head was down, horns at the ready. He'd picked up Lydia's serious tone. 'I suggest you two just put away those guns, and listen to me for a minute.'

John waved them back. 'I'm not moving from this spot!'

'Who said anything about moving?' Lydia said mildly. But she stood firm, Houdini at her side. Dean glanced at the goat and frowned at Steve. Together they backed off a step or two. 'I expect you'd like a word of explanation,' Lydia continued. 'I can see that this must all be rather puzzling. Now, I want you two to go back to Mr Western and tell him this piece of news.'

Steve's lip curled again. 'What's she on about?'

Dean shrugged, but he didn't dare speak. Houdini stared him in the eye.

Lydia drew a brownish paper from her work jacket pocket and began to open it out.

'What I have here is a map of High Cross land,' she explained. 'Dating from the time when my grandfather farmed here. Now, it's an old map but it's a good one.' She beckoned Dean and Steve across. Reluctantly they went and bowed their stubbly heads over Lydia's paper.

'I had some idea that Mr Western and Dennis

Saville might be mistaken,' Lydia went on. 'So I went to my desk the other day and unearthed this map, just in case. See – I was right!' She pointed a finger at a faint dotted line. 'The High Cross boundary cuts across the ridge and down by those hawthorns over there. That means the area where we're standing isn't common land after all!'

Mandy took a deep breath of surprise and relief.

Lydia looked from Steve to Dean. 'You can see for yourselves, it's High Cross land.'

Dean ducked his head and grunted. 'But Mr Western says we have to keep back the rabbits,' he complained.

'That may well be,' Lydia agreed. She folded the map and put it back in her pocket. 'And you have to follow orders whenever you can; I can see that. But not on *my* land, you don't!' She looked calmly at them. 'So you'd best go back and tell Mr Western that from me. Tell him it may not be worth anything as farming land, but I fancy it does rather well as an old-fashioned nature reserve. There's every variety of clover, wild cowslip, and that pretty pale lilac flower which we called milkmaids when I was young. Besides, there's the rabbit nursery.' She smiled at John, then gazed gently round. 'And this is the way I like it, just as it was in Grand-father's time!'

Dean and Steve knew when they were beaten. If nothing else, they didn't like the look of Houdini's sharp horns. 'OK, OK,' Dean said, as the goat stamped and strained at his rope, 'we're on our way. We'll tell him, then he can't blame us.' He muttered to Steve as they backed off; 'It's not my fault if he lives next door to a rabbit lover, is it? It's nothing to do with me.'

Lydia kept on smiling and nodding at John, Mandy and James as the two lads made their way back up the hill, guns drooping, shoulders hunched. 'Well done, Houdini!' she said proudly.

He tossed his head and stamped.

'Is all that true?' Mandy demanded. She pointed to the map bulging in Lydia's pocket. 'How come you made this discovery all of a sudden?'

Lydia's eyes crinkled shrewdly. 'According to this map, it's true; we're standing on High Cross land.'

'But?' Mandy knew Lydia well enough to know there was more to it.

'But Grandfather was an argumentative sort. He had the map drawn up in a dispute against Mr Western's own grandfather. This was over sixty years ago. And as far as I know, the two old gentlemen never settled their quarrel, and the dispute is still in the hands of some dusty lawyer's clerk.' She laughed mischievously.

'In other words?' James said.

'In other words, I don't know whose land it is!' Lydia smiled broadly. 'But those two weren't to know that, were they? And it'll take Sam Western many months to go back to the lawyers and work it all out to his satisfaction. If he can be bothered to go to all that expense over a piece of rough old land like this!'

'Lydia!' James and Mandy chorused together. They hopped around at the success of her little scheme.

Quietly, John bent to pick up his pencil. 'Thank you very much, Miss Fawcett,' he said. he stood awkwardly. 'Thanks, James. Thanks, Mandy.'

His words set a seal on the incident, and now it was plain that he wanted to be by himself again. He sat back on the rock and bent his head over his work.

Lydia nodded for James and Mandy to come away. 'Give him time,' she advised. 'I think that's what he needs.'

That's what everyone says, Mandy thought. *But it doesn't seem to work!*

She and James followed Lydia and Houdini through the long grass. 'He doesn't have any more time,' Mandy told her. 'He goes back to school on Sunday, and I'm really worried about him.' She turned to James. 'You see what I mean about him? It's like he's locked himself up and thrown away the key. I don't think he can ever bear to speak about losing Button and Barney!'

James nodded. They came to a halt in the farmyard.

'What would it take to put things right?' Lydia asked Mandy. 'You know John better than most, I suspect.'

Mandy sighed. 'Button and Barney,' she replied. 'That's what it would take. But they were sold to someone else by mistake earlier in the week.'

They stood together in the dusk.

'I've got it!' James said suddenly. 'If Button and Barney are the only things that'll help, what we have to do is set out and find them, isn't it?' He looked eagerly at Mandy. 'See? If we found the lucky owners and tracked the rabbits down, at least John would know where they were. We might even be able to get them back for him!'

Mandy saw it in a flash; James was right. 'Sometimes I could hug you, James Hunter!' she cried, with a mad urge to fling her arms round him. 'You have the best ideas!'

Lydia laughed as James ducked and darted away. 'Keep her off me!' he yelped.

'Don't worry, you're safe!' Mandy spread her arms wide and spun round on the spot like Superwoman. 'Da-da! Let the quest to find Button and Barney begin!' she announced. 'Pets' Parlour, here we come!'

Eight

James and Mandy were waiting on the doorstep of Pets' Parlour when Geoff turned up looking rumpled and sleepy. It was half-past eight in the morning.

'Hi, it's us again!' Mandy said. 'I bet you wish you could get rid of us!'

He grinned, opened the door and invited them into the shop. 'So what can I do for you this time?' Geoff hung his keys on a hook behind the counter and flicked the switch on a kettle which sat on a nearby shelf. 'Go ahead, talk to me. But don't expect me to take much in at this time in the morning. Not until I've had a cup of coffee!'

'Don't worry, we'll be quick,' James promised. 'We just need a little bit of information.'

Mandy took a pen and piece of paper out of her jacket pocket. She looked up eagerly, ready to scribble down the name and address of Button and Barney's new owners.

Geoff rubbed the top of his tousled head and yawned. 'OK, try me!' He nodded to a middle-aged woman with curly brown hair who'd just followed them into the shop. 'Morning, Mrs Kearney!' he said.

'Can you tell us who took the baby rabbits that John Hardy had bought?' James blurted out. 'You see, he bought them first, so it's him who should really have them, isn't it? And we thought we might be able to track them down for him.'

Mandy's pen hovered over the paper.

Geoff looked doubtful. 'I don't know about that . . .'

'It's OK, we're not planning to go off and kidnap them. Or bunnynap them!' James promised. 'But we did think we could talk to the other buyers and see if they would let John have the rabbits back.'

'They might agree, once they hear the full story,' Mandy put in.

'Maybe you're right.' Geoff frowned and shook his head. 'And I can see that you two wouldn't go and do anything daft.' He glanced again at Mrs Kearney who was just buttoning up her overall, ready to start her day's work.

'Then what's the problem?' James glanced anxiously at Mandy. Their plan seemed to be coming to a full stop before it had begun.

'The problem is, I can't tell you exactly who went off with Button and Barney. These people came into the shop, chose them and paid cash for them. They didn't even give me their name.'

Mandy's hopes came crashing down. She stuffed the pen and paper back into her pocket, at a loss for words.

James was deep in thought. 'But what did they look like, these people? Do they ever come in here for other things? Won't they be coming back to buy food and bedding for the rabbits? Haven't you seen them round town since? Don't you have a clue who they might be?'

'Whoa, steady on!' Geoff held up his hands in protest. 'One thing at a time!' He poured milk into his coffee and stirred it. 'I can tell you what they looked like, but I don't know if it will help much. They were a fairly ordinary couple, a man and wife. I can't say I noticed that much about them. He was tall and well-dressed. She was neat and slim, and well-groomed. I think she was wearing gold earrings. She had blonde hair. His hair was darker, I think.'

'Didn't they have a child with them?' Mandy forced her brain into action, once she was over the first disappointment.

Geoff shook his head. 'No. They wanted to buy the rabbits as a surprise Easter present for their little girl. It was very hush-hush. Apparently she'd been wanting a pet for ages. They were passing by and thought Button and Barney would be just the thing. Easter bunnies.'

James sighed. 'You were right, it doesn't help much. And you're sure you've never seen them before?'

'I swear. But like you say, they might come back for rabbit food and so on. I could always find out more for you then.'

Mandy shook her head. 'No, today's Saturday. John goes off to school tomorrow. We have to track these people down today, to try and get Button and Barney back before he leaves home. That's the plan at any rate.'

All three looked at one another. Mrs Kearney stood in the background, looking uncomfortable. 'Don't worry, nobody's blaming you!' Geoff called out. 'It's just been a bit of bad luck, that's all.'

A gloomy feeling had settled on Mandy.

'Thanks.' Mandy nodded and smiled briefly. 'Thanks for all your help.'

'No worries. Sorry it didn't work out.'

The bell rang as they left the shop. Mandy turned, one foot on the step. 'Oh, we haven't given up,' she promised. 'Not by a long way! This is just a small setback. We've got all day to sort it out!' She closed the door and stepped down on to the street. She breathed in deeply as she zipped her jacket.

'OK, next idea?' James asked. They passed a newspaper shop, Cecil's Confectionery and a chemist's. People queued outside a bread shop, waiting for it to open.

'We could advertise in all the shops,' Mandy suggested. The cards in the newsagents' window had brought this to mind. 'You know; a message in the Wanted section. "Wanted: two brown rabbits from Pets' Parlour. Would the new owners please contact Animal Ark, Welford

703267." If they ring up, we can tell them the whole story.'

'It's worth a try,' James agreed. So they spent half an hour going up and down the High Street, writing out cards and paying to stick them on clear display in all the newsagents' windows and on the notice-board in the town library. 'It's a weekend, so town should be busy,' James said hopefully. 'Plenty of people will read the notices!'

'The trouble is, we don't have much time.' Mandy stood back from the library notice-board. 'What now?' she said with a sigh.

'I suppose we could go over to York. There are loads more pet shops there. We could try them all to see if they've got any brown baby rabbits that look the same as Button and Barney. Then we could go back and tell John we'd found them after all!'

'You mean, *lie*?' Mandy took a deep breath.

'It's only a white lie. And it's for a good cause.'

'I know. But it's a bit risky, isn't it?'

'Shh!' The assistant behind the polished wooden counter pointed to a notice above their heads. It read, 'Silent Reading Area'.

Mandy and James blushed and slunk out of

the library. They stood on the street, opposite the railway station, wondering whether to risk a trip to York. 'Do you think we'd get away with it?' Mandy asked. 'I mean, John is a real rabbit expert now. He's bound to notice the difference. You know what he's like. He probably knows every whisker and hair on Button and Barney's head.'

James sighed. 'You're right. Anyway, I just realised; I spent all my money on those Wanted cards. I couldn't afford to go to York on the train, even if we decided it was worth a try.'

'Me neither. I've only got enough for the bus back to Welford.' Mandy felt another emergency plan flare and fade. 'If only we weren't so short of time!' Tomorrow John would pack his huge suitcase and drag it across the carpark at the Fox and Goose. He'd be off to school, then home again at half-term for the wedding. But there'd be no pet rabbits sitting cosily in his back garden under the apple tree.

'I suppose we'd better go back home,' James decided. 'We've done all we can here. I can't think of another single thing!'

She was forced to agree. 'John will be up at High Cross already, you realise? He'll stay until dark, all by himself, with his rabbits and his sketch-book and camera.'

'I know.' They both sighed.

'I'd like to go and join him, but I don't think I can face him just yet,' Mandy decided.

'It's his last day.'

'I know. But let's go back to Animal Ark first and have one final think about it. I need to tell Jean about our Wanted notices, just in case someone rings up. After that, what do you say we take sandwiches and biscuits up to High Cross? I bet John hasn't even thought of that. He's bound to be hungry.'

James nodded, and they climbed, heavy-hearted, on to the Welford bus. It wasn't often they had to give in where animals were concerned. They could find good homes for kittens, and put up strong fences for goats. They could rescue orphan hedgehogs. But they couldn't magic the twin rabbits out of thin air, and they couldn't make one sad boy happy.

'Cheer up; the holiday isn't over yet, you know!' Mandy's dad called as he climbed into his Land-rover to set off on his morning round. He gave James and Mandy a cheerful wave.

Mandy could hardly raise a smile.

Mr Hope wound down the window and studied her serious face. 'Tell me about it later. Or talk to Mum after surgery. I'm sure we can sort something out.'

Not this time, Mandy thought. She tried to smile back at him. 'Thanks, Dad.' They went inside, to the busy waiting area of Animal Ark.

Toby, Mrs Ponsonby's mongrel dog, came tottering out of a treatment room. He wore a big white plastic cone around his head and looked very sorry for himself. The cone knocked clumsily against the doorpost and he yelped.

'Oh, poor Toby! Poor doggy!' His fussy, middle-aged owner bent to scoop him off the floor. 'Did he hurt his poor little self? Oh, diddums!' She hugged him, and staggered out across reception.

'What's he done to himself?' Mandy stroked Toby gently on the nose. She could see a small, open sore on the dog's back. Mandy knew he had to wear the plastic cone to stop him from nipping at it and making it even worse.

Mrs Ponsonby raised her arched eyebrows from behind her fancy pink glasses and mouthed a secret word: 'Fleabite!'

'Oh, dear!' Mandy sympathised. She knew how they itched. 'Did he go and scratch it too hard?'

'Shh, dear! Yes, I'm afraid Toby was a naughty little doggy!' He wasn't so little. Mrs Ponsonby's legs had begun to buckle under his weight.

'Here, let me help,' Mandy offered. She took the miserable mongrel and set him down on his own four feet. Then she led him carefully out to Mrs Ponsonby's car. 'Don't worry, that wound will soon clear up. It's nice and clean now. It should be better in a few days, then Toby will be good as new!'

'Thank you, Mandy dear!' Mrs Ponsonby stowed her precious dog into the special compartment at the back of her car. She tugged at the jacket of her powder-blue suit to straighten it, then fixed her straw hat more firmly on her head. 'I must say, you're not looking quite yourself today, dear. You're a bit peaky. Is there something the matter?'

'No, I'm fine, Mrs Ponsonby. Thanks!' Mandy helped her to close the back door on Toby. 'I've got a problem on my mind, that's all.' She waved and went inside once more.

On the doorstep, she paused to see who was

turning into their drive as Mrs Ponsonby drove out. 'Oh no!' she groaned out loud. 'Just what I need!'

'Trouble?' Jean asked. She was wearing a flowery dress in white, blue and green, with big white buttons down the front. She looked summery and breezy, but surrounded as usual by a muddle of opened letters, papers, catalogues and bills.

James came across to the door. 'Uh-oh!' His mouth turned down at the corners. 'What are *they* doing here?'

'Exactly!' Mandy's eyes narrowed. She watched as Mr Parker Smythe stepped out of his posh black car and came towards the surgery.

'Since when did they need a vet?' James wondered. Both Mandy and he were only too well aware that the family owned a tennis-court, a helicopter and a swimming-pool. But as far as they knew, they had no pets.

'Hello,' the tall man said. His thinning hair was smartly combed, and he wore a posh grey suit. He looked strict, but he spoke to them pleasantly as he strolled into reception.

Mandy stared hard at his car. Inside, sitting behind tinted glass windows, she spied the blonde head of Mrs Parker Smythe and the chubbier shape of Imogen's pale face. To Mandy's surprise, the girl was actually looking cheerful. She pressed a button to slide down the window, then leaned out eagerly, watching for her father's return.

In the reception area, Jean was talking to Imogen's dad. 'That's quite right, Mr Parker Smythe. Your appointment with Mrs Hope is for ten o'clock. Just bring them inside and take a seat over there. I'm sure you'll be seen shortly.'

Mandy and James slid inside the reception room as Mr Parker Smythe came out. 'Jean, what are they doing here? What's going on?' Mandy whispered. 'I never knew Imogen had a pet!'

'Ah, you wait and see,' Jean replied, smiling sweetly. 'I think you're really going to like these two!'

Soon the surgery door opened again and Mr Parker Smythe backed awkwardly in. He carried a bulky, square shape. Imogen had to hold the door for him to get through.

'Careful!' Mrs Parker Smythe warned from behind in her high, silvery voice. 'That's a good girl, Immi! Let Daddy come right through. Now try not to get too excited, or you'll upset the poor baby rabbits!'

Mandy gasped and held on to the counter for

support. James stared at her wide-eyed. 'Did she say baby rabbits?' Mandy repeated.

'What did I tell you?' Jean beamed at them. 'I knew you'd both gone mad on rabbits lately. You and John Hardy!'

Mr Parker Smythe put the hutch down gently on the shiny floor. Slowly, a brown shiny nose appeared through the hole in the wooden partition of the hutch. Then two brown ears, two bright, shining eyes. One rabbit hopped into view. A second identical one came after.

'Button!' Mandy cried.

'Barney!' James followed her across and they both crouched down by the wire mesh at the front of the hutch.

The two baby rabbits sniffed at their new surroundings and stared out wide-eyed. An ear twitched, a paw scuffed in the straw. They sniffed the disinfected air.

'Like them?' Mr Parker Smythe inquired. He stood back, hands in pockets.

Slowly Mandy stood up and stared at Imogen.

'It was love at first sight as far as Immi was concerned,' he explained. 'Now we can hardly drag her out of the garden to go to bed at night, with these two to look after!'

Mandy took a deep breath. They'd found what they were looking for. But now it was going to take all her tact and skill to get Button and Barney safely back to John Hardy!

Nine

'Hello, Imogen.' Mrs Hope put her head round the treatment room door. 'We're all ready for Button and Barney now. Let's take a look at them, shall we?' She smiled at Mandy. 'Why not get your white coat and come and give me a hand?' she suggested. 'Simon's caught up next door with a spaniel with an injured paw.'

Mandy's head was spinning, but she did as she was told. With clumsy fingers she fastened the buttons on her white lab coat and followed Mr Parker Smythe and the rabbits into the treatment room.

'Can Immi come too?' Mrs Parker Smythe

pleaded from outside. 'She promises not to be a nuisance!'

'Of course she can. Come in, Imogen,' Mrs Hope said. 'Just close the door nice and tight, so the rabbits can't hop about and escape. That's right. Now, let's see what we have here!' Gently she lifted Button out of the hutch.

Emily Hope's calm voice had a soothing effect. Mandy told herself to think straight. Perhaps there was a way of sorting this out. OK, so Imogen Parker wasn't the kindest and most generous person she'd ever met. She probably didn't even know what the word sharing meant. But there had to be a first time for everything! She watched as her mother handed Button over to his new owner and bent forward to take Barney from the hutch.

'I'm glad you've brought them along, Mr Parker Smythe.' Mrs Hope inspected Barney's ears, then gently massaged his bottom jaw to open his mouth. She peered inside. 'Rabbits can easily fall ill with small infections, especially of the eye and ear. They need vaccinations, to be repeated every twelve months or so. The sooner we protect them against disease, the better.'

Barney nestled comfortably in the crook of her arm while she ran her fingertips over his abdomen and chest. She smiled. 'But he's certainly a healthy little chap at the moment!' She gave her verdict and handed him to Mandy. Then she began her examination of Button.

Mandy cradled the lightweight ball of warm fur, holding Barney close against her chest. His round, pretty face stared up at her, ears flat, nose twitching. Her mother began to prepare a syringe, while Imogen took Button and stroked him, laying her cheek against the soft brown fur of his back.

'Shh, Button. No one's going to hurt you! Shh!' Imogen half sang in the rabbit's ear. Her lips were parted in a soft, round shape. She crooned and

stroked her precious pet. Mr Parker Smythe stood back, watching his daughter with quiet satisfaction.

Even Mandy had to admit that this was a new girl who stood before her. The spiteful, selfish child who stamped her feet and swung moodily on her garden swing was gone. In her place was a sweet, loving seven-year-old.

Oh dear! Mandy frowned. How could she spoil Imogen's day by suggesting that she give Button and Barney back to John Hardy? She couldn't just say that they really belonged to John because he was the one who'd bought them in the first place! This was much more difficult than she'd expected.

'Hush, Button, there, there! That didn't hurt too much, did it?' Imogen scooped the rabbit back off the table as soon as Mrs Hope had finished the injection. The tiny creature quivered at the sharp needle, but he soon calmed down under Imogen's gentle touch.

Next it was Barney's turn. Imogen insisted on being the one to hold him too, while Mrs Hope went to work once more. So Mandy took Button from her and put him back in his hutch. He settled quietly into the clean straw.

'It looks like you made a good choice,' Emily

Hope said to Mr Parker Smythe. 'I know that you've been looking around for a pet for Imogen for quite some time. You must be very pleased to have found just the right ones!' She stood back, peeling off her surgical gloves.

'Oh, it's marvellous,' he agreed. 'You should have seen Imogen's face when we gave them to her. It was a picture!'

Oh dear! Mandy took a deep breath. *Why can't life be more simple?* She helped Imogen to fasten the front catch on the hutch. Button and Barney were both snuggled into the straw. This was a situation she hadn't expected to face; either Imogen or John was bound to end up broken-hearted.

'There *is* one thing, though.' Mr Parker Smythe drew Mrs Hope to one side. 'As you know, we've thought and thought about pets for Immi, and often we've decided that we're just too busy to fit them in. You know, I work away quite a lot, and we have a house in Tuscany which we like to visit whenever we can. We'd be there right now, except that I have some business I need to clear up.'

Mrs Hope nodded. She put her head thoughtfully to one side, pushed back a wisp of red hair and listened hard.

'Anyway, we took the plunge with these two rabbits, and we're all thrilled to bits with them both. But I promised my wife that I'd ask you what you thought we might do with them during the holidays. You see, it's quite a problem for us, having pets and travelling about so much.'

If Mandy had been a rabbit, her ears would have shot up. As it was, she sprang upright and stared across the room at the grown-ups. *Maybe . . . just maybe!*

'You want a reliable bunny-sitter?' Mrs Hope considered the problem. 'For school holidays? I take it that Imogen doesn't want to part with them during term-time, when she's at home?'

'Oh, no!' Imogen gasped. 'And I won't ever go on holiday ever again, if it means leaving them all alone, with no one to look after them properly!' She was stung to tears at the prospect.

'Immi!' Her father smiled uncomfortably. 'You know we've already discussed this! You promised not to make a fuss, remember?' He shrugged at Mrs Hope.

'No, no, she's quite right. You do need a good, firm arrangement. So many people just go off and leave their pets without proper food and water, let alone exercise. You simply wouldn't believe it!' She paused, arms crossed, wondering what was the answer. 'But I'm afraid we don't do a boarding service here at Animal Ark. We don't have the space, you see. But we could put up a notice for you. There's a notice-board out in the waiting-room. Perhaps that would lead to something?'

'No need!' Mandy stepped forward. She clasped her hands in front of her to stop them trembling. 'I think I've got the answer!'

There was no such thing as magic in the real world, she knew. But this had just come close. And in an instant, she was about to make one sad boy happy!

Everyone at Animal Ark agreed that it was a brilliant idea. Mandy burst out into reception to tell James. 'Fantastic!' he gasped, rocking back on to his heels. Jean smiled broadly from behind her desk. Even Mrs Parker Smythe looked relieved. 'Are you sure that's all right, Immi? John Hardy does sound like just the right person to look after your rabbits while we're away! And since you haven't decided on names, yet, I think Button and Barney sound perfect.'

Imogen nodded. 'I suppose so.' She cocked her head sideways, looking serious and grown-up. 'And I do like the names.'

Now Mandy was all action. 'Now, let me ring John's dad to see what he thinks,' she said. 'If he says yes, why don't you and Button and Barney come and check to see whether you think the Fox and Goose is OK?'

Imogen thought about it. She peered wistfully into the hutch. 'OK,' she said slowly, her frown easing. 'If you're sure it'll be all right, Mandy.'

'More than all right! John loves rabbits, and he knows everything about them. He'll take really good care of them, don't you worry!'

'When would he have them?'

'Just whenever you have to go away, during the holidays.'

'Half-term,' Mrs Parker Smythe said. 'That would be the first time we'd have to leave them.'

'And maybe tonight?' Mandy asked. 'Just so Button and Barney can get used to John before he goes back to school. Then they won't be so nervous when they go there at half-term.'

'Good idea.' Mr Parker Smythe had relaxed. The crisis was over. He wanted another quick word about the rabbits with Mrs Hope before they left.

Meanwhile, Mandy reached for the phone to explain everything to the Hardys.

'I'm sorry, Julian's not in,' Sara said. 'And John's up at High Cross, of course!' She had listened carefully to the news. 'But I think it's an absolutely great answer to the problem. I tell you what, let's keep it a secret from John. You bring the rabbits over here for this trial run, and I'll find somewhere to hide them for when he comes in. I just want to see his face when he discovers them. It'll make his day! Well, it'll change his life, as a matter of fact. Thank you so much, Mandy!'

The phone clicked and Mandy went ahead, making sure that Imogen was happy with all their plans. 'Thanks for letting John have Button and Barney for tonight,' she told her when they had reached the Fox and Goose. 'I know it's hard for you to let them go.'

'Yes, but they will be all right, won't they?' Imogen was trailing after her father across the pub carpark. She watched anxiously as he took the hutch in through the back garden.

'Come in, I'll show you,' Mandy promised. 'Sara said she'd find just the right hiding-place for them; somewhere secret where John won't spot them when he first comes in. Come on, let's go and see!'

They went upstairs, along the crooked corridor, into John's room.

James and Mandy went in ahead of Imogen, who hung back. Then she crept in behind them and stared round at the walls covered in photos and sketches; dozens of rabbits, hundreds of rabbits; close-ups, long distance, at play or feeding. 'Where are they?' she whispered. 'Where's Button and Barney?'

'In here!' Mr Parker Smythe called out. 'Through this door. What do you say to this, Immi? Bunnies in the bathroom!'

He held the door open wide and pointed to the two little brown rabbits peering curiously round the white tiled space. 'Satisfied? Now let's say goodbye for now and leave Mandy and James to settle them down. We can come back and collect them early tomorrow. That's a good girl; I'm very proud of you.' He took her by the hand.

Imogen sniffed. Her mouth puckered. She bent down close to the hutch. 'Goodbye, Button! Goodbye, Barney! See you tomorrow!' She whispered.

By teatime, Mandy and James could hardly bear

to wait any longer. They were certain that John would stay up at High Cross until dusk; another two or three hours of unbroken suspense.

'Let's go on up there!' James suggested. 'We could persuade him to come down early.'

'No way!' Mandy bit her lip. 'He won't come until the very last rabbit's disappeared down its burrow. It's his final day. Wild horses wouldn't drag him away!'

'OK. Anyway, he'd probably suspect something.' James sat down again on the grass in the pub garden. It was a clear evening, with a tint of pink in the sky. Dusk tonight would be long and late.

'No, we just have to wait.' Mandy sat cross-legged under the apple tree. White blossom drifted on to the grass. Glasses clinked and customers chatted in the bar. 'Anyway, Button and Barney are both asleep.'

'Well, they've had a busy day.' James leaned back on his elbows.

Soon Sara brought out a tray of lemonade and crisps. 'Julian's just got back from town,' she told them.

'And?' Mandy got to her feet. 'What's he say?' Surely Mr Hardy wouldn't object to the new plan; not after all this!

'Come here!' Sara waggled her finger at them.

They crept indoors and up the stairs. Inside John's room, Mr Hardy was busy fixing big white display boards on to steel frames. He wanted to arrange his son's sketches and photos into an artistic display before John came home. He turned quickly and saw them peering in.

They lent a hand, pinning up the pictures, making sure they were straight. But it still wasn't even dusk by the time they finished. Mandy glanced at her watch, then at James.

Mr Hardy stood back to judge the effect of their work. 'Do you think he'll like it?' he whispered. 'It's a big surprise!'

Mandy and James nodded. 'It's not the only one!' James added.

'Thanks for your help,' Mr Hardy whispered. 'Now why don't you two scoot up to High Cross and meet up with that son of mine. Tell him I said it was time he got himself back home. But don't let on. I want everything to stay a complete surprise!'

Ten

John sat on his low rock by the nursery warren. His sketchbook lay across his knees. His camera still had its lens cap fixed firmly in place. He sat in the fading light. All around, the rough grassland dipped and rose; hazy green, alive with rabbits.

'Shh!' Lydia warned. She came out of the house to walk with Mandy and James across to the far pasture. They were ankle-deep in grass and buttercups. 'I've had my eye on him all day, poor little mite. It breaks my heart to see a boy so alone.'

'Let's wait until the rabbits have gone in before we interrupt him,' James whispered. They came to a stop by the low wall and stood watching.

Mandy longed to run across and send the rabbits scattering across the hillside. She wanted to run up to John and give him the good news. But she kept her promise to his dad. They studied the mist rising slowly from the valley. It crept amongst the trees, over the patchwork fields. 'Has there been any more trouble with Dean and Steve?' she asked Lydia.

Lydia gave a wicked little smile. 'Not a squeak. Sam Western, their boss, came to see me though. According to him, the old land dispute was settled in favour of Upper Welford Hall. In other words, John over there *is* sitting on common land!'

'But?' James prompted.

'But I didn't let him get away with that, let me tell you!' She laughed. 'I told him to go and check his facts with the Land Registry. Meanwhile, he'd better keep Dennis Saville and his lads off *my* land!'

Mandy grinned. 'Phew!' Mr Western was known as a loud-mouth and a bully. He wasn't popular, but he did have friends in high places.

'Don't worry.' Lydia stood, hands in pockets, collar turned up. 'That man's a stickler for laws and lawyers himself. He won't dare send men out here with their guns while there's a question mark over who owns the land. When our friend John comes back home in a month or two, I guarantee he'll still be able to come up to this warren and find it just as it is now. Peace and quiet; that's what we like.' She breathed in deeply and threw her shoulders back. 'Peace and quiet!'

At last the light faded from the hill. The mist rose and the rabbits went to ground. John sat on in the damp twilight.

Mandy glanced uncertainly at Lydia.

'Go on, you two. It's time for you all to go home. You go and fetch him now.' She smiled at them both and said goodbye. 'Take care of that young man for me, and tell him there's a cup of tea for him at High Cross any time he cares to drop in!' She wandered off across her field, back to the house.

John looked up at Mandy and James as they trudged through the wet grass towards the rock. He uncrossed his legs and tucked his sketchbook under one arm. 'Hi,' he said in a flat voice. 'It's OK, I've finished here. I was just about to come down.'

'Your dad says you have to come home,' James told him. 'They say you've been up here all day.'

'Well, they don't have to worry about that now,

do they? After tomorrow I'll be gone, and they'll be alone together, just those two!'

'Oh, I don't think they want to get rid of you,' Mandy put in. 'In fact, I'm sure they don't. They've been really worried about you since—'

'Never mind!' John jerked to his feet. 'Anyway, it was a waste of time you two dragging yourselves all the way up here. I was on my way without needing to be told!'

Mandy nodded and kept her head down. John was in no mood to be friendly. They walked silently across the fields, making their way through the mist, guided by fence-posts and trees, until they reached the lane leading down into the village.

'It'll be dark before we get back,' James warned. 'Or just about, at any rate.'

Mandy and he chatted on about Lydia's goats, about school on Monday; homework they hadn't done and friends they would see. John walked in silence, locked away, lost in his own thoughts.

He didn't even notice when they walked on past the crossroads with him, instead of turning off to their own houses. He walked on through the village, head down, his dark figure striding two or three steps ahead. James and Mandy jogged the final stretch to catch him up. They entered the pub garden together.

They were greeted by the buzz of customers drinking in the bar. It sounded cosy and warm. But John went straight upstairs, not knowing or not caring that the other two still followed. His door stood open. He went in, unzipped his jacket and flung it on the bed with his sketchbook and camera.

'Surprise!' Mr Hardy stood with one arm round Sara's shoulder. He revealed the new gallery of John's work, waiting for a reaction.

John hesitated and blinked.

'What do you think?' His father came forward. 'Do you like it?'

'Yes, thanks, Dad, it's great.' John attempted a smile, but his voice gave him away. 'But you shouldn't have gone to all this trouble.'

'No trouble,' Mr Hardy said uneasily. 'Don't you think they look really professional? We'll have to talk about you taking it up as a job when you leave school.'

John shrugged. 'I don't know.' His own rabbits stared silently back at him from every angle.

Then Sara came forward and took him by the hand. 'Surprise number two,' she said gently. She

led him through to the bathroom.

Button and Barney had done what all rabbits do; they'd woken up to feed and play as night fell. They bobbed and hopped about inside their hutch, which rested on two planks of wood, carefully placed across the width of the white bath. As John approached, they hopped forward to the wire mesh, and poked out their noses in greeting.

'Carrot?' Sara offered. She handed two pieces to him.

He took them, too stunned to say anything. Button and Barney curled back their lips to show their long front teeth. They waited for their treat.

Mandy watched as John's blank face broke into a smile. The rabbits set to and nibbled. He crouched there with all the patience in the world, waiting until every scrap of carrot was gone.

Then he stood back. Without saying a word, he went up, put his arms round his father's neck and buried his face in the soft blue wool of Mr Hardy's best golfing sweater.

That evening they celebrated. John dashed downstairs to consult Ernie Bell about building a wire run for Button and Barney. 'Can it run the length of the whole garden, so they have lots of space to come out and feed?' he wanted to know.

Ernie sipped his beer. He winked at Mandy. 'Oh, aye, I reckon it can.'

'And will it be strong enough to keep them in, so they can't escape?'

'Aye. I'll make it just like the run I made for my Sammy, only not so high. Sammy, being as he's a squirrel, likes to climb a bit, see.'

John nodded. 'Rabbits like to dig. They won't be able to dig their way out, will they?'

'No problem. I'll put a good barrier along each edge, well dug in. Matter of fact, I've already promised one to the Parker Smythes up at Beacon House. It looks like I'm going to have my work cut out.'

John backed off, satisfied. Button and Barney were going to live in the lap of luxury in both their houses.

Walter Pickard, sitting across the table, tutted. 'I don't know, young man. You'll be wanting one of them Jacuzzi things for them before long!'

'Rabbits don't like water!' John laughed.

'Aye well, then, it'll be an 'utch with a patio and a sun umbrella!'

Mandy got up to go. 'James's dad has just arrived to give us a lift,' she told John.

'Yes, and I've got to go and pack,' he said. 'And check up on Button and Barney, of course.'

'Don't worry, they'll be OK,' she grinned. 'They're probably fast asleep again.'

'Thanks to you,' he nodded. He breathed a deep, happy sigh. 'I'll be back in six weeks. Ernie says the run will be ready by then.' He looked away, scratched his ear and gave a dry cough. He was blushing as he turned back to her. 'Er, Mandy . . .'

'What?' She saw Mr Hunter and James hovering by the door. 'Look, John, I've got to go!'

'Will you write to me?' he asked in a rush. 'Tell me how Button and Barney are getting along up at Beacon House. I mean, it's OK if you don't want to; you don't have to!'

'Of course I will!' she promised. A smile swept across her face. 'Any excuse to go and visit those bunnies!'

'Rabbits!' he said sternly. 'Er, Mandy, do you think you could manage to write to me, say, once a week?' he stammered.

'Twice!' she promised again. 'Three times! Whenever there's any news!'

'Oh, thanks!' John had turned crimson to the roots of his hair. 'Now I know it's not going to be half as bad!'

As it happened, John wrote first. A letter fell on the mat at Animal Ark on the Tuesday of the following week. Mandy was still in her pyjamas, with slippers wet from going out across the dewy grass to feed her own rabbits. She yawned as she opened the scribbled note:

Dear Mandy,

How are Button and Barney? Have they settled in at Beacon House? Tell Imogen not to feed them too much lettuce; it's too rich for them to have every day. I got an A++ for my project. Sorry if that sounds like boasting. I hope James is OK.

Love, John
P.S. Don't forget to write back soon about Button and Barney.

She wrote:
Dear John,

Button and Barney are fine. Ernie's started to build the run at Beacon House. But guess what? We all made a mistake. We thought Button and

Barney were both boy rabbits. All right then, male rabbits. But Mum says we were wrong. Barney's a male, but Button's a female! Mum says she's absolutely sure. There's no doubt about it.

Mr Parker Smythe wanted to book Button into Animal Ark for her operation. But Imogen wants them to have one litter of babies first. (Sorry, kittens!) Her mum and dad said yes. So guess what again? Button and Barney could have babies soon! Isn't that great? Just think – baby Buttons and Barneys! What could be better?

Love, Mandy

He wrote back a one-line letter:
Dear Mandy,

Great news. OK, so I guess I don't know every-thing about rabbits!

Love, John.

The Animal Ark Newsletter

Would you like to receive The Animal Ark
Newsletter? It has lots of news about Lucy
Daniels and the Animal Ark series, plus quizzes,
puzzles and competitions. It is published three
times a year and is free for children who live in
the United Kingdom and Ireland.

If you would like to receive it for a year,
please write to:
The Animal Ark Newsletter,
c/o Hodder Children's Books,
338 Euston Road, London NW1 3BH,
sending your name and address
(UK and Ireland only).

ANIMAL ACTION

If you like *Animal Ark* then you'll love the RSPCA's Animal Action Club! Anyone aged 13 or under can become a member for just £5.50 a year. Join up and you can look forward to six issues of Animal Action magazine - each one is bursting with animal news, competitions, features, posters and celebrity interviews. Plus we'll send you a fantastic joining pack too!

To be really animal-friendly just complete the form – a photocopy is fine – and send it, with a cheque or postal order for £5.50

Registered charity no 219099

(made payable to the RSPCA), to Animal Action Club, RSPCA, Causeway, Horsham, West Sussex RH12 1HG. We'll then send you a joining pack and your first copy of *Animal Action*.

Don't delay, join today!

Name ....

Address ....

....

Postcode
....

Date of birth ....

Youth membership of the Royal Society for the Prevention of Cruelty to Animals

AACHOD2